The Blind Alpha's Pregnant Mate

Talia Swarky

Published by Talia Swarky, 2022.

THE BLIND ALPHA'S PREGNANT MATE

First edition. January 18, 2022.

Copyright © 2022 Talia Swarky.

ISBN: 979-8201254988

Written by Talia Swarky.

Also by Talia Swarky

Supernatural Soulmates
Overdue
A Goddess Born
Twins, Tentacles, And Other Squirmy Things
Brandi's Brownie Baby Surprise
One Full Moon
Triple The Surprise
Quick Beats
Popping On The Birthday Stream
The Best Experiment
The Blind Alpha's Pregnant Mate

Watch for more at https://books2read.com/ap/nBkZpK/
Talia-Swarky.

Table of Contents

"DOMINIC, I SWEAR TO God if you don't quit drinking all my booze, I'm going to chop off your fucking lips!"

The tall man currently draped over my barstool didn't even blink, flashing one of those panty melting saucy grins that all my pack member's loved, and raked a hand through his mess of short strawberry curls. "Come on, Kit. It was just a little tequila. Maybe a bottle or two. You know I'm good for it." His nose wrinkled up at the tip in that way that made his ginger freckles bleed together, stifled a burp into one thick fist, and tossed a wink of his olive-green eyes my way.

I sighed, waddling my way over to his corner of my bar, and snagged the neck of the empty glass bottle with two fingers. "Just because you're the pack's Beta doesn't entitle you to special treatment like this." Adding a little extra oomph of agreement, my baby kicked low against my hip, making the tight fabric of my black 'Rock on!' T-shirt faintly shiver with the movement. It made it even more obvious because I was 5'4 and all belly, like I had a supersized watermelon growing straight in my belly.

Dominic's hazy eyes catch the movement, subtly widening at the corners. "Damn, that kid looks like it's going to bust right out of there. You sure you've still got 4 weeks to go?"

"Yep, and that's just an estimate. Usually the babies in my family run late, like my mom said I was about 2 weeks overdue." Giving my stomach a little pat, the baby settled right back down... for now. Currently standing at 36 weeks pregnant, my little passenger was a little more active than my doctor said was usually normal, but I assume that it was because the full moon was approaching soon. Of course, the doctor was assuming that I was having a human baby, but it's a werewolf, just like me and its father.

Bracing one hand against my back, I shuffled back to the storage area through the kitchen, and plopped the empty bottle right into the crate of tequila that had just arrived this morning. It was a good thing too, with the full moon approaching in a few weeks, my packmates would be on edge and I'd need all supplies on deck. So what if the doctor said I should take some time off? I can't stand to sit on my ass and wait around for something to happen, I need to have something to do or I'll drive myself crazy.

Plus, it didn't give me time to think about *that*.

A soft jingle, and the sound of heavy footsteps crossing the scuffed wooden floor quickly faded into a soft hum of conversation. I stretched my senses to the limit, tipping my nose up high in the air, and briefly closed my eyes as the wolf senses came to the fore. Wood, and smoke. Oak. That's what it was. Fresh Oak, like someone had been running in the woods, but it was tempered with the sharp clean scent of fresh rainwater and something else. Something uniquely male and very strong. My scarlet painted lips started to stretch into a smile, Tyler. That was Tyler's scent. I knew it by heart. I had for years, even when we were three years old and he gave me half of his PB&J because a few bullies stole my lunch. My Alpha.

Letting my fingertips drift over the smooth glass bottles, my mind tracked back to our conversation this morning where he said that he was going to be out with a couple of the pack today. Something about the scent of an intruder out on the fringe of the territory, and I wasn't stupid. Since I was the most vulnerable member in the pack right now, that's why I hadn't been able to shake Dominic off my ass today. Annoying he may be, but he was still our pack's Beta and second in command. Not to mention that his lethal combat skills could make most wolves show their belly in five seconds flat.

Plucking out a full bottle, I had started to turn for the door when I caught sight of my reflection in the mirrored surface of my stainless-steel refrigerator. Short, choppy layered hair dyed a bright bubblegum pink hung just across my ears. The five-inch strappy leather sandals curling around my slightly swollen ankles, and the black pleather leggings showed off every curve of my legs. Including the slightly wider span of my hips and ass. My shirt was still clinging to my belly, showing off the bulge of my navel and the new larger cup size of my swollen breasts. Plus, the music bar tattoo that ran down the inside of my right arm was peeking out, and the words believe in yourself under my right wrist slightly caught the light. Combined with my perky, slightly upturned nose, and the too thick cat eye frames keeping my stormy gray eyes in focus. I looked like a punk rocker whale that had beached.

I sighed, shaking my head, and turned away. Following the tangled burr of conversation out into the main area, the full force of his aura hit me before my foot ever cleared the door. Like a warm blanket sliding around my shoulders, it was protective and comforting in the same way, but without being annoying. Standing across from Dominic with his arms crossed across his broad chest was Tyler Ferguson, the Alpha of our Thunder Ridge pack.

Tall, and leanly muscled, his long jaw and sharp chin combined with the low light of the bar created beautiful shadows, the kind that highlighted the dimple in his cheeks and the cleft in his chin. The dark aviators kept his eyes hidden, but my spine arched automatically when he twisted to face me, his nostrils flaring slightly as he registered my presence.

Then, like warm caramel flowing from a jar, a crooked smile curled his lips up. "Hey, Kitty Kat! I was waiting for you."

2

Tyler

"DON'T CALL ME THAT!" Kat snapped, and I chuckled. Just as feisty as always, her heels clunked against the floor as she walked towards us. The vaguely peppery scent of her soap swirling through my head and mixed with the slightly sweet scent she carried these days. I won't lie, it did a wonder for the migraine trying to crack my skull open, and the tightness in my chest finally started to ease.

"Are you feeling bad today, Kat? Usually you can take a little teasing." I tipped my head to the side, focusing on the sound of her quick tripping heartbeat and the echo of the baby's much faster but softer tone. They sounded normal, but something was bothering her. The dim light in the bar wasn't helping my legally blind vision out much, reducing the normally fuzzy haze of things I could see to a shifting curtain of moving shadows. My lips pursed slightly, the rough edge of my teeth subtly gnawing on the lower rim, and the slight pain was a little reassuring.

"You'd be irritable too if you had this idiot shoved up your ass all day." The slight rasp of her clothes shifted as she clunked over to the furthest edge of the bar, the sound of clinking glass echoed through the air, and the solid whump of a door closing was punctuated by the firm press of her hand.

"Hey! I'm right here!" Dominic mumbled, the thick rank of booze clinging heavily to his breath, and I felt his body shift and lurch towards mine. I stepped back, idly watching the impression of his blurry body fall completely off the stool. "Ow!" He landed with a hardy thump, the plain tile floor shaking softly underneath my feet, and I shook my head with an amused grin.

"Did you break anything?"

He was quiet, too quiet with just the noisy rasp of his breathing, and I started to get a little concerned until I heard him shift. "No."

"Then go on out and give me a minute with Kitty Kat. I need to talk to her *privately*."

"Alright, alright." He mumbled in a strangely complaint tone. His body thumped and rolled, scrambling to his feet with so much noise that if anyone passing by heard him, they might think he was a bear stuck in a dumpster. "I'm outta here!" His voice drifted on the stale air, preceding the dull thump of the door as it slammed shut. There was only one reason why Dom would agree so easily, instead of pestering me so badly that I wanted to slam my fist in his face, and that was if he was planning something. Maybe I'd just be lucky today, and he had a new girlfriend that he wanted to see.

"Finally! If I knew it was that simple to get rid of him, I would have called you out here a long time ago." Kat sounded harsh, but I could tell she was laughing. Her voice always had the little squiggle at the end when she did. Now that Dom was out of the room, the air had started to still except for where Kat was moving around. Cozy actually, and maybe it was just from spending all morning running through the woods, but this big wave of exhaustion just slammed right down on my bones like a tidal wave.

"Dom was just keeping an eye on you like I asked, so he's not entirely to blame for his actions." Tucking the folded length of my cane into the hip pocket of my jeans, I took a seat at the nearest stool and propped my elbows up on the bar. Silence greeted me, but I had a feeling she was rolling her eyes at that. "Don't roll your eyes, they'll get stuck backwards in your head."

"Oh, shut up!" She said with a giggle, an honest to God giggle, and my mission was accomplished for today. "Did you find the rogue?"

Mission not accomplished. Scrubbing a hand against my cheek, the rough edge of stubble coating my jaw reminded me that I hadn't shaved this morning, barely taking time to hop in and out of the shower before joining Kirby in the forest before the sun was ever up. Six fucking hours of running our legs off, following the sickening soured scent of filthy body, and nothing but a dingy little campsite with a dead fire and a few ashes to show for it. "Nothing but a put-out campfire. We circled the entire town for hours, and there was nothing else but that. He's here somewhere, but somehow he's disguising his scent."

She was quiet again, too quiet, and it made my hackles want to rise up. I narrowed my eyes, listening to the restless shuffle of her hands across the counter. "So what? Do we just sit around and wait for him to show back up?"

"I didn't say that." Okay... that was strange. She spun on her heels, the sharp steps quickly taking her to the opposite end of the bar. I couldn't shake the feeling that she was hiding something, but what? We've had rogues before; it's just they usually didn't try to hide themselves while on our territory.

The sweet scent of fresh milk snapped me right out of my thoughts, my exhausted wolf instantly stood on alert, ready to shift at the first sign of danger. Jamming my hands into my pocket, I pulled out my cane and snapped it out to full length, making my way down the bar and avoiding the tables scattered around. "Kat? Are you okay?" Leaning forward until the counter edge jabbed in towards my stomach, I reached up and pulled off my glasses, squinting towards the wobbly blob of a figure that was squatted down at floor level. Her heartbeat spiked, a sudden hissed in breath, and she cursed low under her breath as her clothes rustled.

"I'm fine. Just started this damn leaking again. And I don't have time to change for my doctor's appointment." She hissed, reaching up to grab something off the top of the counter. "I guess I'll just have to go with my top milk stained and say I spilled something on me."

"It's an obstetrician, right? They're probably used to it by now." Letting my fingers wander over the counter, I found the tissue box I knew normally sat right beside the beer taps, and pulled out a few. "I'll call Gina and she'll go with you; she might have an extra top you can wear too."

"I can go by myself, thank you very much." She whipped the tissues right out of my hand so fast that my fingers burned. "Just because I'm pregnant doesn't mean I'm helpless."

I sighed, tucking my glasses into the neck of my shirt and gave her my best Alpha glare. The blurry blob of Kat swayed up with a heavy grunt, shifting her weight to one foot, and waves of anger pulsed around her like some kind of prickly aura. "You're not helpless, and I would dare anyone to attack you unless they wanted to lose a hand. But the fact is that you are pregnant, very heavily pregnant, and that makes you our most vulnerable pack member. If you don't want one of the others to go with you, then I'll go. It's that simple."

She started to argue because it felt like my skin was on fire from the weight of her gaze, but then she stopped when a different little buzz started to ring out. Kat swore loud and hard enough to make a sailor blush, slamming her hand down and the buzzing silenced. "Fine, let's go! I don't have time to argue with you."

3

Kat

I SIGHED, KNEADING my knuckles into the aching side of my ribs while a cold draft drifted from just over my head. It wasn't helping that the baby had decided to use that moment as practice for their future runs, kicking their feet all up and down the front of my belly until it was jiggling like a bowl of gelatin. "Easy in there! I'm not a bouncy house." I muttered under my breath, smoothing one hand against the upper curve of my belly and using the other to lean back on my elbow.

"Is there anything I can do to help?" Tyler arched an eyebrow, tipping his head to one side while his hands restlessly smoothed over the folded length of his cane. With the way the morning sunlight was streaming through the one window in the room, it was too easy to see his pulse jumping hard and fast in his neck, a visible sign of the quick thud of his heart echoing in my ears. That was odd, Tyler was never nervous, not with any of us like this. It made my wolf want to snarl in frustration, my skin already starting to itch with the change wanting to bloom. Did that rogue wolf really make him that nervous, or did he just not like being in doctor's offices?

"No. Just try not to talk too much. It gets the baby excited." Tyler's hands flexed again, my gaze briefly flicking down to see the skin across his knuckles was bone white. My hips were throbbing from the pressure of sitting on the hard table so bad that it felt like I was about to pop. Shifting my gaze around the room, the wooden cabinet, plastic diagrams, and all the other medical stuff was stored just opposite where I sat, topped by a little square metal clock that was slowly ticking away each second. How long could it take for the test results to come back? The nurse had already swabbed everything ages ago, and it felt like I'd been in here for hours. I sighed again, the baby taking that moment to kick my kidneys with a sharp foot.

9

"I know, I can hear the baby swirling inside you." He chuckled softly, a warm sound that made my heart swell and my mind go blank.

"Really?" I glanced down at my stomach, watching the little ripples of movement roll under my shirt. I hadn't thought much about it, but werewolf hearing is pretty sharp, and anyone could probably hear all the movements of my little ninja. It's not like it wasn't obvious, considering how big I am, but it's probably even louder to Tyler since he's sensitive to sounds. "That's just what I didn't need to know."

Tyler leaned back in his chair, crossing one long leg over the other and settled his hands and cane in his lap. "It's not that much of a big deal, it's a part of you and I've learned to separate the difference between the two of you." A flash of white teeth teased against his tanned skin, one thick brow arching up with silent laughter. "The little one doesn't complain nearly as much."

"Oh, shut up!' My cheeks flushed red hot, both of my arms cradling my twitching belly like I could muffle the sounds. The baby agreed with him, quickly rolling around until my stomach took on a slightly lopsided shape. I "Here, give me your hand and you can feel just what you caused." I waited a moment for him to stick his hand out so I could take it, but he didn't.

Instead, his broad shoulders straightened so sharply that it looked like someone had jabbed a steel beam beneath his skin. The twin dark eyebrows knitted together, dipping down into a dark v with sudden refusal. "No, it's fine. I don't want to make you uncomfortable or anything." I wish I could see his eyes behind those damned glasses, just long enough that I could tell what he really thought, but his posture said that something was off. Really off.

That's when it hit me that out of our pack, Tyler is actually the one person who hasn't really felt the baby at all. Maybe once or twice, but that was about it. Considering that he normally touches things so frequently, especially when he was working on his wood sculptures. It was very odd to hear him refuse it. "You're not going to hurt me. I want you to feel my belly."

He hesitated, quickly twisting his head towards the door, and I watched as his jaw flexed sharply. Like some kind of rope had tightened between us, the easy reassurance he always had suddenly vanished, replaced by this cold empty air that made a shiver rippled over my skin. Finally, with the glacial slowness of one of those sloths on a nature program, he stood and flicked his cane out to full length, tap-tapping his way over the five steps separating us and held out his left hand.

His fingers were warm and strong, lightly calloused from all those years of shop work with the power tools, and very stiff as I raised my shirt and guided it across the drum tight bulge of swelled skin. He let out a shaky breath, trying to slightly pull back from my touch, but I flattened my hand over the top of his. Keeping it pinned right there above my bulging navel, the baby gave a little answering thump from deep within and rolled. Tyler jolted so sharply that you would have thought I'd shot him, and I couldn't keep in the snort. "It just surprised me, that's all." He muttered low, leaning forward as he slowly started to relax and let his fingers do the talking.

"Fine by me, just as long as you keep that up. I'm a happy girl." God, it felt like heaven! The warmth of his rough palm felt so good as it spread out completely, his fingers twitching as my hand dropped away to let him explore on his own. He shifted forward, frowning in deep thought, and traced over every inch of my massive belly. Starting low at the base by my hips, and mapping all the way up to the curve just under my breasts, it felt like I was one of those sculptures he creates for people and he was smoothing away any imperfections. Planting both hands behind me, I arched my back and let my head fall onto my shoulders, pushing my belly out for as much of his exploration as he wanted to give. I wasn't the only one that was enjoying it too, the baby rolled right into his touch, following Tyler's every movement, and I watched through slitted eyes as a slight crack of a smile twisted up his lips. I wish things had turned out differently, because I could definitely get used to this.

A rough rap of knuckles raked across the door, and it broke the moment like someone had dropped a vase. Tyler stepped away, retreating back to the safety of his chair, and I quickly tugged my shirt back into place just as Doc Wilson's smiling face popped in the door. "Well, hello there Ms. Wade! How are we doing today? I see you've brought a friend. Are you the father?"

I choked right there before I could answer, my tongue trying to dive down to my stomach, and Tyler tipped his head to the side in curiosity. Did he know? He couldn't know. I'd tried too hard to keep it a secret. "No, I'm just along for moral support today."

"Well, that is perfectly fine." The doctor walked over to the cabinet, pulling open a drawer and taking out a pair of medical gloves. His smile widened, the lights glimmering off the broad expanse of his bald head, and my stomach tossed around like I was about to upchuck the contents across the floor. "Everything is picture perfect, Ms. Wade. All of your tests came out just fine, and now I'd like to proceed with your exam, if you don't mind."

"Go ahead," It was easier than talking about the potential factor of who my baby's father might or might not be, and seeing the innocent confusion flash across Tyler's face. I leaned all the way back, pulling my shirt up beneath my breasts, and let the full mound of my belly jut up towards the ceiling. The cool air raised a slight shiver across my skin, but it was nothing compared to the icy cold touch of the doctor's hands as they traveled across my belly. My teeth bit down against my tongue, the small pain momentarily distracting me from swatting him away as he gently pressed in to make sure that the baby was growing like it should.

"We're still laying quite high, aren't we?" Doctor Wilson said to my belly, his fingers pressing in on the top of my uterus just under my breasts. "And quite large too. If the current position is any indicator, I suspect that you won't be going into labor anytime soon. Possibly even going later than most, and we may have to induce you." He finished with a small pat to my belly, and an answering thump back from inside told me just what my little passenger thought about that.

The rustle of fabric to my left drew my attention over to where Tyler was shuffling slightly in the chair, leaning forward to catch every movement as the doctor moved away and snapped off his gloves. He pitched them into a small metal trash can sitting just at the corner of the cabinet, stepping out of the room just long enough to roll in a large machine on a cart. Topped with a large computer screen that was wide enough to fit on my apartment wall as a TV, Doctor Wilson didn't waste any time slathering the icy cold gel all the way across my belly, and pressed the scanner to the underside of my belly. My chest tightened, my heart racing like it was going to break out of my chest. This was the part that always scared the crap out of me. The insistent hissing of static rolling through the speakers until one sound gave away.

Th-Thump Th-Thump Th-Thump

There it was. My baby's heartbeat galloping along like a little motor. An easy smile split my lips open, my gaze fixed on the screen where the full figure of my baby quickly appeared. It wriggled, one hand raising up like it was waving back at me, and I squeaked out a laugh so sharp that it felt like my throat was breaking open.

"So far, we still look good. But let me get a few more angles." As Doctor Wilson pushed the scanner around my belly, I hadn't noticed how tightly that my hands were gripping the sides of the table until a set of strong fingers wove through mine. Squeezing gently, I turned and Tyler flashed a reassuring smile that loosened the rest of my fears. "Everything looks great, Ms. Wade." The doctor removed the scanner and turned off the monitor, the sudden silence in the room like someone had thrown a blanket over us all. Pushing the cart away, he handed a few tissues to Tyler and pulled a notepad from his pocket. "Ms. Wade may need a little help cleaning up, but I'm sure you can help her, and I'll get the prescription for your vitamins." He nodded with a smile, and then he was gone.

It took a moment for me to understand what he meant by helping me clean up, but it became abundantly clear when Tyler swallowed heavily and stood up, tapping his way to my side with the tissues clenched tightly in his right hand. But then it hit me like a truck, and I struggled to say no when I really wanted to say yes.

4

Tyler

"SO, UM... DO YOU MIND?"

Not the most intelligent thing I've ever said, but the soft snort that came from Kat said a lot. "Go ahead, if you can get under my belly, that would be great." As much as it killed me to admit that I hated the thought of another man's baby in her belly, there was something so magical about feeling it move. The firm warmth of her skin, the twitches of little limbs moving inside, it was so hard to believe that she had that little pulsing life inside her, but here it was. The rustle of clothes shifting caught my ear, and I squinted to see the blurry form of Kat lean back and bare her belly to the air.

Rounded out like a watermelon and speckled lightly with the pink stripes of stretch marks, with the fat little nub of her navel pushing out like a turkey timer. She flinched slightly when I dragged the napkin over her belly, the sticky metallic scented gel easily cleaning away with a simple touch. "How's that?" I whispered low, trying to disguise the hint of rasp that had creeped in my throat.

"Feels great." She straight up moaned. The heat of her skin easily bled through the napkin and straight to my fingers, the twisting firmness of the baby pushed out against my hand, and I chuckled low in my throat. That was cute. I bet she was smiling, it sounded like it. A second burst of her intoxicating scent hits my nose as she wriggles, one hand rising up to tug around the area of her breasts, and it's tinged with a hint of something else. Something musky and familiar, and it makes me hard in a heartbeat.

"Sounds like you are enjoying it."

"If you felt like your belly was so tight that it was about to split open, you'd enjoy a little rub too. Ahh..." Her spine arched, pushing her belly even more into my touch as I moved higher up, dragging my

15

fingertips over the swollen upper curve. It was tight, she wasn't lying about that, and I wonder if there were other parts of her that were just as tight. My fingers were barely making a dent in her hot skin, and the baby continued to wriggle under the tensed muscles of her stretched womb. I licked my lips, heart racing in my chest, and framed both sides of her belly with my hands. Adding in a shift of my thighs to try and hide Mr. Happy that was threatening to rip through my jeans, I hope she didn't glance down, and that her wolf senses weren't kicking in right now.

Kneading both of my hands in against her sides, her keens and moans turned up a level. Quite pants and jerky breaths shook her sides, and I could hear the rustle of the sanitary paper covering the table against the back of her head as she tossed it back and forth. Her scent hit me again, thick with the sweetness of her arousal, and the warmth of her body against my hands felt like it snapped whatever balance had been between us.

The muscles in her belly tensed, her body pulling itself up with far more strength than I realized, and the pink ring of her hair shot up into my sight. "Come here!" She growled, all wolf deep, and my breath caught in my throat as she curled one hand around my neck. Her lips slammed into mine, soft and plump with the faint taste of cherry from her lip gloss, and she moves hungrily at first but then softens. I don't take time to think, parting my lips and letting my tongue swipe out against her lower lip, and she opens up like a flower. A hot wash of heat floods my veins as I raise my hand and curl it around the back of her head, the soft short strands of her hair weaving through my fingers, and the cane clattered to the floor, instantly forgotten.

It felt like I was on fire, everywhere her hands touched, my shoulders and my back, it burned. She must have felt it too, her hips lifting up off the table to throw her legs around mine, and she pressed herself as close to my cock as she could, adding an extra grind that made my eyes fly wide open right before the door popped.

We sprang apart like rubber bands snapping, my cheeks burning red hot and I really couldn't breathe. My head was swimming, the floor and the ceiling all mixed up as I dropped to my knees and ran my hand over the floor, searching for my cane and trying to figure out how she stole my lungs out of my chest. "Sorry to interrupt." A polite lady stepped inside, the soft scuff of her sneakers crossing across the floor didn't hide the smile in her voice. She knew what had happened, I'm sure. "Here's your vitamins, Ms. Wade."

"Thanks," Kat panted, still out of breath, and she groaned as her spine popped when she shifted forward. I didn't dare look up, not until I reached under the bed and the smooth edge of my cane greeted my fingertips. Good, I had that back under control at least. Now for my brain and my cock to reverse each other's blood flow.

"We'll have the bill ready and waiting for you out front." The lady said, and I raised up just in time to catch both of their shapes combined together like one melted blur. She must have been helping Kat down from the table. Yep, her short little legs hopped down, and her arm shifted to cradle the underside of her belly.

"You can just send the bill to the Thunder Creek Pack fund, handled by Alex Garcia." I popped out before Kat could say anything. Her head shifted, and I could feel her glare searing my skin, but I smiled politely and stood up. "Will that be a problem?"

"Oh, no. Not at all." The lady chuckled softly, murmuring something I didn't catch to Kat, and stepped out of the room.

"What the hell was that? 'Send the bill to the Thunder Creek pack fund'?" Oh, crap. The hiss of her voice sounded like a snake, and she waddled my way with one finger poked towards my chest like a mini sword. My hands flashed up, pulling my cane crossways across my chest, and her finger and her belly smacked into my body at the same time. "I can pay for my own care myself! Why do you think I work every single day?"

"Kitty Kat-"

"Don't call me that!" That finger prodded my chest, right over my heart.

"Kat," I tried again, narrowing my eyes to show her I was serious. "I don't know what all happened when you were with that pack up north, but here. I always make sure that one of our own is taken care of, and that includes the both of you."

"Oh," She dropped her finger, her head tilting to one side as stepped back. The sudden absence of her heat left my skin chilled, and my mind started screaming at me to pull her back and kiss her, but I didn't. Instead, I stretched out my cane and waited until she was through gathering her things before following her out of the room.

What an idiot!

MY HEART WAS STILL pounding when I slammed through the door and out onto the sidewalk. The cars zipped by on the street, blasting my face with the rush of gas scented air. It felt like razors slicing my skin, rubbing my already raw nerves into a shocking pain, or maybe that was the baby that had decided to use my left ribs as a punching bag. I groaned, the repeated stab stab of tiny fists felt like a knife was cutting through my bones, and heaved my tote bag up on my left shoulder. A quick glance down confirmed just how visibly my belly was jiggling, the pointed outline of a small arm pushing the entire bulge off to my right side, and clearly outlined by the tight fabric of my shirt.

"I hope you know that part of this is your fault." I said, smoothing a hand over the bulge and feeling an answering punch directly to the center of my palm. If the baby hadn't got so excited, then Tyler wouldn't have rubbed my belly, and this led to that. And if we hadn't kissed, I wouldn't be wearing my extra set of spare underwear I kept in my tote for leaks because the ones I had been wearing were wet as all hell right now. Horny pregnancy hormones had almost made me push Tyler right down on the bed and ride him until I couldn't breathe, and then he just had to pay for my doctor visit too? If he wasn't such a good guy and my best friend. I'd deck him.

"So, you thought you could hide from me?" A silky voice slinks out of the shadows, and every instinct instantly flares up. My hands clenched into fists, my hips shifting back into a fight stance, and my eyes burn as they shift from gray to wolf gold. It's like everything turns up a notch, the sights and the scents, and something extremely sour floods my nose so hard that it makes me gasp. That's not just anything sour, but the kind of sour like when someone hasn't washed for weeks. "You can't hide from your Alpha."

"What the hell are you doing here?" Shit fucking hell! He was supposed to be rotting in jail somewhere in Boston, not here. A quiver of nerves pooled in my stomach, and suddenly my wolf was aching for backup. Tyler's kind of backup, and how long could it take for him to take a shit?

Something circled around my back, the squish of soft footsteps, and I spun on my heel. A muscular wrestler's body, doubled up with beefy arms and thick corded legs, was topped with a large head and crowned with a thin fringe of dishwater blonde hair. His golden eyes bulged from their sockets, red rimmed and feral, and the smirk that drops his gaze to my belly chills my blood into ice.

"Ronan, I told you to stay away from me!" The wolf's growl pours out of my throat as I start to edge back towards the door, but he speeds away. Blurring so quickly that I can't see him, my instincts scream at me to run away. A fist aims for my head, and I rock back, letting my weight push me away but a second blow catches me on the chin. My legs staggered, a kick snapping out my left leg, but an arm circled around my throat.

"You can't hide this from me." He rubbed his wide hand slowly over my belly, almost lovingly if a beast like him could feel love. Fear curled around my spine, churning in my stomach and threatening to rip up my throat as he made a second pass from the base of my belly to the top. His fleshy lips lingered on my neck, pressing the edge of his blunt teeth into the junction of my shoulder like a soft mating bite. "Both of my babies, right here. We were good together once, we could be again, Kat."

"Get a life, bozo! We're over!" I snarled back. My jawbones cracked, the bones lengthening into the bulging snout of a wolf muzzle, and I clamped down on his arm. A salty flood of blood gushed into my mouth, the tug of my teeth embedding into firm bone shakes my head, and his screech of pain makes me flatten my ears as they stretch out into wolf ears. Ronan's grip loosens slightly, letting me wriggle free. My left arm arched up, slashing open his belly with the claws sprouted on my fingertips.

"You bitch!" Drops of spit flew from his lips as he hissed, clutching his arms over his blood-soaked stomach. The crimson stain spreads through the dirty fabric like water, but it's quickly sealed back off as his flesh knits back together. Werewolf healing at its best.

"I told you when I left the pack. I never want to see your ugly face again, I was stupid to even let myself fall into a relationship with you, and we are through! Or do I need to use smaller words so that you can understand me?"

He blinks a couple times, his tiny brain struggling to keep up even as his face darkens to a brilliant crimson. He's angry, the veins standing out on his forehead like small snakes, and his hands grind into the fabric of his shirt like he's aching to destroy something. Anything, and I'm just the closest target.

"You've got a lot of nerve trying to attack a member of my pack. Why don't you crawl back to where you came from, *rogue*. The lady said that she didn't want to see you, and I certainly didn't give you permission to enter my territory." Tyler's voice, soft as silk but layered with steel underneath, crept out like a whisper and I watched with wide eyes as he slid between me and Ronan. I hadn't even heard him come out, but he folded his cane up and tucked it into his back pocket, rolling his shoulders back and leveled a playful smile in Ronan's direction. "So why don't you just beat it like a good puppy?"

Ronan eyes shoot between Tyler and me, something cold and cruel calculating in those wolf eyes, and he bares his teeth in a cruel smirk. "This is what you left me for? A helpless gimp that can't even see you? What can he do to someone like me?"

"The best I can." Tyler smirked, and before Ronan could blink, he moved so fast that I could barely see him. A jab to the solar plexus, another straight to the belly, and a punishing knee jab to the balls topples the brawny wolf like an imploded skyscraper. A quick strike to the neck finished him off, and Tyler is barely breathing hard as he glares down through his shades at the now unconscious wolf. "Kat, you okay?" He murmured; his fists still coiled like the triple year boxing champion he was through college.

"Yelf, finz." My words came out garbled, distorted all to crap from the combination of half formed wolf muzzle and tongue, and I pushed the change away and the bones snapped back into place. The taste of blood didn't go away that easily though, the iron taste still clung to my lips, making my tongue want to shrivel up and dive back down my throat just to get away from it. It felt so vile, like oil or something. That's what it reminded me of, a piece of roadkill I had tasted in wolf form once. "I'm fine," I repeated a second time, pushing my glasses back up my nose.

"Good," He stiffly bobbed his head. "Send Dom an SOS text, he'll alert the others-"

With a blood curdling howl, the tote handles slid from my shoulders and my arms curled protectively around my belly. Ronan pushed himself up on his elbows like some kind of wrath, his eyes flaming with pure anger, and charged directly into the street. Tyler whipped right behind him, only three strides behind when his head snapped to the left. A car, it's motor roaring fast and hard, barrels down the street at a breakneck pace. It easily swerves around the other traffic, the hot tires squealing against the asphalt, and there's no time for it to stop. I lunge out, grabbing Tyler's arm before his legs can swing out, and pull him back as the car barrels through the space where he was just standing, two tires briefly jumping up on the sidewalk.

"Fucking hell! What was that?" He curled his arm around my shoulders, pulling me so tight against his chest that I could feel his heartbeat racing against my collarbone. "Who was that?"

I watched the cars surge by, completely eliminating any trace of Ronan that might have been left behind. "Someone I used to know."

The whisper popped out before I could stop it, and that familiar trickle of uneasiness curled around my spine.

6

Tyler

IT WAS LATE, ALMOST midnight, when I finally dragged my sorry ass home and into bed. The cool, if slightly stale air, of the room felt pretty damn good against my skin, chasing away the sweat after running around the perimeter of town, but the still... How the hell had that rogue managed to weasel his way straight into downtown Thunder Ridge? And worse, lurking behind Kitty Kat's obstetrician. How had he known she'd be there, and what had she meant by he was someone she used to know? Was he the baby's father, or something else? "There's too many damn pieces here!" I snarled, raking both of my hands through my hair. How long would it be before he tried to find her again? Working whatever plan he had come up with against her?

I rolled over, reaching to the left side of the bed for my pillow and buried my face in it. The soft clean scent of the soap was so soothing, pulling apart some of the frazzled knots in my nerves, and subtly reminded me of something else. The soft cologne that Kat had taken to wearing since she was so sensitive to scents. The same cologne that had clung to her warm skin, and even to her hair. God, she had been so soft, even with her belly so tight and full, she was still soft. The familiar stirring in my core started to tightened, and I muffled a groan into my pillow even though my left hand was already dropping down.

She had let me touch her, and kiss her. It felt like a fucking dream, but she had. The taste of her lip gloss still clung to my lips, and the memory had branded itself in my mind. She was so eager, seeing how hard I got for her, and that was the worst part. She could fucking feel it when she was grinding on me right there in the fucking doctor's office.

Shame crawled down my spine as my hand slipped down to cup my bulge, stroking my thumb over the head, and it feels like my jeans are made of iron. Off. They've got to come off! My hands are shaking, barely able to pull the zipper until it sprang apart with a hiss. A deep groan left my throat, the instant relief from the pressure was great, but it ached at the same time.

Her lips, letting out one of those groans like she did when my hands were kneading her skin. They were so plush and full. Warm like her skin, my left hand slid around my cock, quickly sliding into the strokes like it was her own lips that were cupping it. She'd tease me, drawing it out to the tip before plunging back in. Yeah, that's what she'd do, and I could feel every inch of that smirk of hers pressed against me. Fully hard now, I flopped over onto my stomach and pushed the pillow down against my hips. It wasn't nearly as soft as her body, but it'd have to do.

"That all you got, Tyler?" Her voice would quaver at the end, split by her quick breath shaking out of her chest as her fingers dropped down, playfully teasing my balls with the edge of her nails. Easily gliding under my touch, she'd lean forward and let my fingers roam as they explored every inch of her lush body. Her breasts would be full and firm, the sweet-scented milk leaking from the tips of her rosy pink nipples each time my thumbs rolled across the firm tips, and my hand curled in harder. Stroking faster, hot sweat starts to spread across my palms, mixing with the precum and the slap of wet skin sounds obscene, but it's the kind that stokes the fire in my gut.

The telltale pulse starts low, then moves higher, shifting my thoughts into something darker. It's her walls instead of my hand that's holding me now, keeping me captive in her slick warmth as she slides down to the hilt. One of my hands would weave through her hair, the short strands so downy soft despite as they slid through my fingers. Maybe I'd tug a little and she'd moan, arching her chest towards my lips as I bucked my hips to meet hers. My thrusts turned ragged, my jaw falling slack as the lines between dream and reality blurred.

With a gripping, I cum so hard that it leaves me breathless and shaking. The sticky fluid drenching both my bed and my hand as it overflowed from my cock and dripped down my thighs. The overwhelming scent of musk scratches at my nose, making my eyes water, and just for a moment I could believe that she was still here. Still calling my name.

Actually, someone was calling my name. My eyes flared open wide. The dull thud of footsteps outside my door pulled me out of my haze, and I shook my head, trying to clear out the fog from my senses. Dom's steps, the heavy, foot flopping gait that sounded like he was crushing a houseful of termites with each step was unmistakable.

"Yo, Bro. We've got news." He knocked on the door twice, roughly pounding his knuckles against the wood. "Sammy spotted the rogue when she was out for her run. Hanging around the gas station on the edge of town. He disappeared when she gave chase though." He paused, the air thickening with a hint of mischief. "You through in there, or do you need a little more 'alone' time?"

"Yeah, coming." Shit! He'd smelled it. I should have known. The bedsprings squeaked as I rolled over, groping across the bedside table for something to clean up with, and a soft papery fabric brushed my fingertips. Ah-ha! Tissue! That works. Swiping up as much of my cum as I could with the tissue, I yanked the sheets off and bundled them up for the wash, grabbing a pair of shorts out of the drawer as I passed by.

He leaned there against the door as soon as it opened, one arm raised up high over his head, and the blurry features of his face contorted into a smile. "Have a good time?" He chuckled.

"Shut up!" My face blushed so red that it burned. I could just slap him right now, but I turned away and started climbing down the steps with the bundle of sheets wedged against my hip.

"And miss this golden opportunity dropped right in my lap after you gave me all that shit about my own lady friends' habits. No way in hell!" He stomped along behind me, the steps shaking under my feet like it was an elephant instead of a wolf. "Why don't you just tell Kat that she is getting you all hot and bothered? She'll probably enjoy having a good fuckbuddy."

"In case you haven't noticed, Dom. She's pregnant." I stopped in mid step, shifting the sheets around in front of my belly in case his sight was worse than mine. "And she would probably try to chop off my dick if I even made a move towards her. Some ladies don't like being touched while Pregnant."

"You know an awful lot about this pregnancy stuff." He shot back, and my cheeks fired up full blast again. How could I respond? That as soon as the first whiff of her hormones hit me, I barely stopped myself from cumming in my pants right there? That each day I want to go over there and plead with her just to let me touch her once? That as her pregnancy grew, I scoured the internet for every single piece of information I could just to try and find out what would make her the most comfortable. What I said before was true, a lot of women didn't feel comfortable sexually in their pregnancy, but there were also a lot of ladies who did. She was my best friend, and under no circumstances would I ever dishonor her in any way, even if this morning's evidence seemed like she firmly fell in the second category.

"What did you learn from the other packs?" Shifting gears as we reached the bottom, I slid my hand along the wall until the bulge of the light switch flipped up. The faint orange glow of the lights flickered on, illuminating the living room/ kitchen combo of the condo we shared. It was small by most standards, the giant 72-inch tv was on the left wall, and surrounded by a large sofa and two recliners on either end. The small kitchen with the attached laundry room was just off to the right, and I skirted around the overstuffed leather sofa with well-practiced ease, striding into the kitchen and making my way straight to the washer.

"I made a few calls around, and nobody is reporting any missing members. There is a rumor about a pack to the north having some power shifting going on, but that was it. No mysterious strangers, or anything. Does Kat have any idea why he's after her?"

"She said that he was someone she used to know. That's it, but he scared her pretty badly. She didn't say anything else on the way home." I had left my pack member, Sammy, to guard Kat, and I wasn't concerned about the rogue getting to her as long as she was there. Being that she was a police detective with a 100% accuracy rate with her handgun, and a werewolf on top of that. The muscle-bound freak would be hard pressed to get through Sammy if he wanted to harm Kat, but still. I scowled, opening the washer lid and dumping the clothes inside, something just didn't fit. And there was that north connection.

Just what had happened to Kat when she lived up north?

I COULDN'T SLEEP WELL that night. Knowing that Ronan was out prowling around, every bump and knock in the night felt like it was him trying to sneak into my house. The baby was anxious too, restlessly rolling around with my belly constantly twitching. I rolled over onto my left side, the mound of supportive pillows still keeping me slightly tilted up towards the ceiling, and cracked open my crusty eyes to see the blaring numbers of 12:06 a.m. I sighed, scrubbing a hand through the sleep spiked strands of my hair. I might as well get up and get a drink of some milk or something. It might help me sleep.

My thumb soothingly rubbed into the small bulge of butt sticking out of my left side, the baby's soft twitches swirling against my ribs made me smile, and I swung my legs over the side of my bed. The room spun for a moment, the weight of my belly briefly pinning me down, but I kicked again and pulled myself up. Snatching my glasses off the table beside my bed, my hips started to ache as the full weight of my belly pushed down on my legs, and I braced one hand under the curve and started waddling out of my room.

It wasn't far, but it felt like the longest walk in the world. Since I had moved back to Thunder Ridge, I had moved in to share a 2-bedroom apartment with my roommate, Sandy Carpenter. A tall buxom blonde built like a supermodel and the sweetest heart ever, she never said a cross word to anyone, and sometimes I couldn't stand it the way guys generally treated her like a dishrag. It actually wasn't just guys, but everyone in general. If someone wanted her to cover a shift at the restaurant she worked at despite her already working a 6-hour shift, she'd do it with no complaints. I really needed to talk to her about resting again, I was just exhausted looking at her.

Speaking of, I heard the sound of high heels clicking up the steps outside, and the door opened. Standing in the hall across from the bathroom, I flipped on the hall light and her watery blue eyes squinted up like I'd just spotlighted her. "You work a double again?" I said, waddling past her to the opposite site of the apartment and the small kitchen to the left.

Sandy sighed, dropping her heavy messenger back on the table beside the door with a heavy thunk, and pulled the scrunchie out of her thick curly brownish blonde hair. Her burgundy work shirt and black dress slacks were splattered with a rainbow of food stains, and a smear of reddish sauce trailed down her left freckled cheek. "Yeah, I just... couldn't turn down my coworker when he said that his aunt was in the hospital and needed him right now." Something else was about to come out, but her jaws parted wide in a lingering yawn.

"Uh-huh. And was this the very same coworker that said last week he needed you to cover his shifts because his car broke down and he couldn't catch a ride to work." Arching one eyebrow high, I threw a glare her way and opened the fridge. The cool air instantly soaked through the thin fabric of my nightshirt, my nipples hardening so quick that it left my heavy breasts aching, and the baby kicked hard against the front of my belly. A soft grunt leaked out of my throat, and I reached in and snagged the remains of the spiced curry chicken I had made last night. The plastic bowl easily slid into my hand, and I popped off the lid and took in a deep breath, the spicy scent making a low growl curl up through my stomach. "You want a bite to eat?" The click of Sandy's heels followed behind me, and I turned back around to see her holding one hand tight against her belly and the other to her lips. Her cheeks paled, and she stared at the bowl in my hand like I just offered her poison.

"No thanks," She muttered, the words muffled by her hand. Slinking backwards a few steps, her hand continued to awkwardly rub at her stomach like she was trying to soothe it. Snagging a fork out of the drawer, I propped my left hip against the counter and pierced a sauced piece of chicken on the end when it hit me. I used to rub my belly like that during the earlier stages of my pregnancy. My eyes flashed up, quickly taking notice of the way her shirt buttons were straining to stay closed over the small pudge of her belly. God, I was so stupid!

"You're pregnant!" I blurted out, and she froze. Her eyes stretched so wide that I thought they would pop out of her skull, and both hands instantly folded over her belly. "Who's the father? Is it that jackass who keeps standing you up?"

"No! It's just a guy I met at a bar a month ago. After my cousin's wedding. I thought I was okay, but I found out last week I wasn't." A single tear trickled down her cheek, and she looked down at her belly. Her hair slid around, covering up most of her face, but I could still hear the little snuffles. That, and now that I was more focused on her than my own noises. I could hear both her and the baby's tiny heartbeat pounding away.

"Do you have any way to contact the father? You've got to let him know."

"No! I never got his name!" This fact made the tears really start flowing down her cheeks, and she shifted her gaze from her own flat belly to mine. "And you're one to talk. Not letting that Tyler guy know that your baby is his, or did you finally tell him?"

"Hell no!" How could I? He'd never forgive me, and he obviously doesn't remember us having sex. So how could I even start that kind of conversation? I stabbed my fork into the bowl, picking up a huge bite and shoving in my mouth until my cheeks bulged like a hamster's.

Apparently being pregnant had already kicked Sandy's hormones into gear because she swiped away her tears with the back of her hand and stabbed one finger towards me. "Look, just because I'm the fragile little human and I don't understand all this big bad wolf stuff, it doesn't mean I don't smell shit when I see it. You need to tell him, *now*. Before that crazy ass ex of yours decides to do something worse."

"Wait, wait, wait! You know about my ex? How?" I threw the bowl into the sink, forgetting just how hungry I was in favor of pushing myself back fully on my feet. Propping my hands on either hip, I wobbled forward a step and until my belly brushed her hip. She jolted back like I had burned her, instantly dropping her eyes down to the floor, and mine started to burn like they were changing over to gold. Scratch that, my gums itched and split, the wolf fangs popping through at just the thought of Ronan's ugly mug. "Spill it." I snarled, my voice rippling with the edge of a growl.

Her heartbeat kicked up double time, and her breathing turned shallow as she pointed one trembling finger towards the pile of envelopes resting in a small basket partially hidden by the toaster. Normally the place we dumped the assorted junk mail until one of us felt the need to go through it for anything that we might be interested in, the sharp edge of a small square package poked up from the nest of white rectangles.

What the hell?

I crossed over, snagging the basket with one hand and easily grabbed the package up. It was small, perfectly palm sized, and taped across the top. I flipped it over, looking for a return address or any indication of where it had come from, but all it had was my name and address across the top. "What the hell did you do?" I muttered softly to myself, shaking the package and hearing a small rattle from inside.

"Who's it from?" The half-muffled words were mixed with loud wet smacks, and I glanced over my shoulder to see that Sandy had pulled a jar of hot fudge sauce from the cabinet and was steadily working her way through it with a spoon.

"Someone you really don't want to know." A swirl of dread tightened my chest, and a kick from the baby to my stomach made me want to barf up what I had just eaten, but I walked to the drawer and pulled out a knife. Quickly slicing through the tape with a single stroke, the flaps of the box parted like an unfolding flower, eager to show off its contents no matter how much I dreaded it. Nestled inside in a cradle of white tissue paper was a small rubber pacifier and a yellow note, each item deceptively innocent, but there was not a doubt in my mind on the identity of the sender now.

The baby started to really roll around, throwing my belly into a leftward slant, and pushing out as far as it could. I winched, drawing in a hiss through my teeth, and smoothed one hand under the fabric of my shirt. It didn't help much, the baby continuing to push out like it wanted to break me in half. Maybe it could sense the package. "Kat, are you okay?" Sandy asked, but I couldn't speak. My tongue was too knotted up, and I swallowed hard against the dread gathered in my throat, and reached out to unfold the note.

The fragile paper parted easily with my touch, fully opening to let me see three large words printed in a bold, blocky style.

SEE YOU SOON

"Sandy," I drawled, my heart pounding about five hundred miles an hour. "Hand me my phone. I've got to call Tyler."

"WE'VE GOT THE PLACE surrounded, both in wolf and on two legs. If he's hiding anywhere, we will find him." Standing in the dark outside Kat's apartment building, it was hard for me to make out the shape of Dom's face, but his voice said it all. Dark as midnight and sharp as steel, the familiar click of the small pocket knife he carried sliding in and out of its case thickened the air. The tension pulled tight, slamming through my shoulders like an iron bar and pulled back. My brother rocked from one foot to the other, the soles of his shoes squeaking like anxious rubber ducks, but he waited for my orders.

"Good," I said curtly, nodding my head in his direction, and turned to stalk towards the door. The bright light above the entrance to Kat's apartment building brought a small bright spot to the misty dark clouds that formed the rest of my vision, reflecting off the smooth glass doors that guarded the interior. One good punch and they could easily be broken, and it wouldn't even take wolf strength either. Or if he wanted, the fire escape wrapping around the building would be an even easier access point. Of course, he could always just leap across from the next building over, head down from the roof, and boom. He was in. Damn it, there were just too many possibilities.

"Hey, heads up to your left." Dom's warning brought me out of my thoughts just before the solid presence of his hand dropped onto my left shoulder. I flinched, fighting back a growl, and turned to see the hazy outline of his face half illuminated by the light. "Don't worry. If we see one toe of this asshole, he'll be rolled over on his back quicker than you can blink." He paused; one side of his jaw tilted up in a lazy smirk. "Go on up and check on Kat and the baby. I know you're dying to."

"Shut up!" My cheeks burned, and I aimed a swat in his general direction. He dodged back with ease, cackling all the while, and wandered off into the distance to join the others. My lips curled up in a smile despite the fact that I wanted to punch him into next week. Stupid idiot!

I sighed, raking a hand back through my hair, and tipped my head up to squint at the fuzzy outline of her building. Kat lived on the 4th floor, and I'm sure she wasn't relaxing at all. Making my way inside and to the inner stairs, I could smell him everywhere, clinging to the steps, and the banister. A deep growl rumbled through my chest as I passed the first level and started climbing up, the click taps of the end of my cane bouncing off each step was much more even than my pulse. Gliding up over the side of the wall, I ran my fingers over the little braille sign that marked each level from the other. The number 4 formed itself under my touch, and I headed for the door.

The hallway was just as empty as the stairwell, the chatter of tv's, people talking, and other noises mixing together like a mushy lump of dough, and I pushed all those noises to the background as I walked to the end of the hall. The door opened before I ever reached it, the tall frame of Sandy, Kat's roommate, stepped out to meet me.

"Tyler, I'm so glad you're here." Her voice shook slightly at the end, her arms folding around her chest. The scratchy sound of her blouse rustled with the movement, a cloud of soft powder scented perfume floating up, but there was something else. I tipped my head, letting the scent soak in, and lurking just under the surface was the sickly sour scent like Kat used to have. Oh, yeah. That's right. I forgot that her roommate was pregnant too. "Kat is very shaken up, but she won't admit it. And she won't let me do anything for her. And I think she's having contractions, but she won't tell me, and I don't know what to do!" She sounded frazzled, the tumbling ups and downs of her voice were making me sick to my stomach like a roller coaster.

"Don't worry, I'll take care of her. You just go and get some rest." A little of the anxiety pouring off her body lessened slightly, and she heaved in a deep sigh before stepping back and let me in. Their apartment was pretty small and very dark, and I kept my cane out and tapped around since when I had visited their apartment, I had the unlikely habit of tripping over whatever shirt or pants they had dropped on the floor. Sandy continued to flutter around as I walked down the hall, her quick movements bouncing off the walls like a quicker echo of my own. Kat's scent grew stronger, mixing with the sound of her sharp quick breaths partially muffled through the door. My stomach flipped over, fear instantly pooling so loud in my belly that I felt like I was going to be sick, and I swapped my cane to my left hand and brushed the knuckles of my right across the wood. "Kat? Can I come in?"

It seemed like forever before she answered, the moments stretched out by the sound of my heart beating in my ears. "Yes," It finally came, broken at the end by a sharp hiss, but it was all I needed. The smooth wood slid under my hand as I reached down for the doorknob, my eyes squinting down through the dark gloom to barely make out the oblong shape of the handle. The cool metal greeted my fingertips with a welcoming chill, unlocking with a quick flick of my wrist, and the door opened with a gentle push.

The musky scent of sweat and fear hit me like a punch in the gut, the entire room so dark that I couldn't see a damned inch in front of my nose, and I shuffled one foot in front of the other. "Kitty Kat?" I ventured tentatively, twisting my head left and right as my senses tried to sort where the echo of her breath began before it bounced off the walls.

"Here, on your left." Another sharp breath hissed through her teeth, and a pair of squeaky bedsprings screamed in protest as she shifted her weight. Ah! Gotcha! I tapped my way to the left, taking easy steps until something solid bumped into the wide swings of my cane.

The bed rustled as she shuffled again, the sound of her breath and fast heartbeat jolting the last clinging strands of the confused fog clinging to my senses, and everything kicked in razor sharp. "D-Did you find anything?" A rare tremble catches her voice, and I reach out and pat the bed with my palm before taking a seat.

"Not yet, but we will." The bed squeaked, dipping sharply under my weight, and the feel of her body heat warmed my arm. She didn't say anything at all, but her breathing started to even out some, a slow breath slinking between the quick ones. A restless urge returned to my hands, wanting to just do something to help, but I settled on folding my cane up and placing it next to my right thigh. "Is that all he sent you? Just the pacifier and the note?"

"Yes." A soft groan slipped out, and the bed dipped and shook as she shifted again. She sounded worn out, and my hands curled under into the fabric of my jeans as she cursed under her breath. Sandy said that she thought she was having contractions, and the baby was due anytime now. If that bastard put so much stress on her that something happened to either one of them, I'd make sure that his mangy ass would regret it for the rest of his days.

"Is there anything I can do? Like rubbing your belly again? Or maybe your back?" Letting one hand crawl across the bed, I found her knee and patted it softly, not wanting to add any more stress. But her lips smacked loudly as she considered it.

"Anxious to cop a feel?" Just like before, her tease made my cheeks turn flame red, but it wasn't as effective when she growled under her breath. An impression of a shape against most of the room darkness hunched over, curling around her belly, and it broke the last of my nerves. I dropped to my knees by the side of her bed, feeling my way to her legs, and pushed my chest against her knees.

"Easy now, just relax." Her belly was hot beneath the silky fabric of her shirt, the muscles shifting and twitching beneath my fingers in time to the frantic rhythm of her pulse. My heart started to pound harder and faster as I laid both palms wide on either side and started to move towards the center. Taking in wide strokes from her ribs to her navel, my thumbs made small circles in any places that were extra tight with tension, or with the wriggles of the baby. She seemed to enjoy it, some of the tenseness leaking out of her frame, and she relaxed so far that her spine arched, letting her belly spill out into my hands. "That feel good?"

"What is it that made you so good at giving massages? It can't be the whole blind deal?" A soft thud came as she let her arms fall back against the bed, the subtle vibrations coursing up through my elbows.

I shrugged, rubbing down a straight line from the upper curve of her belly down to the base at her hips. "Blindness, being a sculptor, I live through what I feel through my hands." Blinking slowly, I gazed up through my lashes at the dark smudge that should have formed her face. It must have worked, because her body jolted with a quick inhaled breath that jiggled her belly. Her stomach twisted again, not from contractions but from the baby letting out a quick thumb against my palm. Curious, I tapped back, and the baby did it again. "This is amazing." I murmured softly, chasing the movement with my fingers, and my heart swelled up like it was going to break my ribs.

It probably wasn't one of my better ideas, but a sudden urge seized hold of me so strongly that I couldn't fight it. I bent over, letting my lips brush over the extended nub of her navel and kissed her belly. Her body shook, jolted by the small gasp and sucked in, tucking her skin around the swollen mass of her womb.

"Tyler," Kat said slowly, a huskiness deepening her voice to a dark rasp, and the sudden warmth of her hand lacing her fingers through mine startled me. But just for a moment until she lifted my hands higher, resting my palms up on the higher curve of her belly. The air grew thick and heady, tinged with her musk leaking up from the v of her thighs, and it made my heart pound in time with hers. "We can't. You're my friend." Her protest wasn't very strong, like she was teetering on a glass wall herself, but it was enough.

If she had kicked me in the heart with one of her stilettos, it would have hurt less. My heart twisted and sank down to my stomach, drowning any sparks that wanted to stir to life, and I drew back on my knees and gave her a stern look. "You need something to distract you, and that would help with both the contractions and taking your mind off that asshole rogue."

"Oh, don't worry. I couldn't forget him if I tried."

Okay... maybe this was a bad idea all the way around. "Who is he? Is he the father of your baby?" I barely managed to choke out the words, each one stuck in my throat like a bad bone after a hunt. A subtle pulse of my wolf awakening rolled through my veins, sending a surge of restless energy pulsing down my spine. *Kat was one of my pack, not this rogue's.* It seemed to say, *And the pack protects its members from harm.*

She snorted again, making a harsh sound in the back of her throat. "He could dream of it, but there's no way in hell that it would happen. He's not the father, don't worry. He's just a pack member when I lived up north who I dated a few times, and didn't get the clue when I said that I never wanted to see him again. I didn't use small enough words apparently."

That was a relief, but it did lead to another question. "Kat, if he's not the father. Then who is? Not that it matters to me, it's your private business. But if he does show up and wants to claim the baby, I want to know so that we can be ready."

She was quiet for a long time, so quiet that I could hear their heartbeats and the soft pops and rattles of Sandy's movement in the next room over. She stroked her belly, the soft dry rustling of skin sliding over skin came with the slight gurgles of the baby stirring inside. "The father is a wonderful man, someone I really loved, but he doesn't really know about the baby. There are certain things in our life that didn't keep us together, and that's okay. I still love him the same, it just won't work out." Her jaws parted wide in a yawn, the muscles and joints clicking as they stretched to their limits. "I'm feeling really tired now, and I've got to get up early in the morning for work."

"Oh, I'll let you get some rest then." Standing up, I traced my hands over the bed until I found my cane laying right where I had left it. My pinkie brushed her thigh, just enough that I felt the tingle of her touch, and sent every bit of those sparks flaring to life again. My arms ached to hold her, to chase away her worries, but all I could manage was to step back towards the door and give her a small smile. "If you need anything, I'll be out here on the couch for a while. Just give me a howl."

The end of my cane had just brushed past the door when I heard the bed squeak. "Hey, Tyler." She called softly, and I turned around with one eyebrow raised high in question. "Thanks, for everything." It was partially muffled, maybe pushed into her pillow, but I heard every word.

"No worries. Just try to get some rest, okay?" There were still more questions that I wanted to ask, but I stepped out into the hall and closed the door behind me with a soft click. At least now it was quiet, Sandy's soft snores coming from her own room, and I settled on the couch. My mind refused to stay quiet, running through every speck and nugget that Kat had tossed my way, and it made my headache just thinking about someone else trying to come and take the both of them away. A grumpy punk hedgehog in wolf form basically described Kat, but I couldn't imagine losing her either. Maybe tomorrow we could find that rogue and get rid of him for good.

9

Kat

THE MUSIC WAS PUMPING, surging in my veins like someone was playing the bongos, and the liquor was flowing like water. A nice cold beer and a whisky on the rocks seemed to be the favorites of the crowd tonight, mixed in with a few margaritas every now and then kept my bartender busy while I pulled mugs of beer from the tap. Usually, the Friday Night Lights band night kept things hopping, but this was really busy.

A particularly loud boom of an electric guitar came from the stage, jolting the baby into poking its butt right in the upper center of my belly, and battering my stomach with a flutter of angry kicks. A heavy wave of nausea crashed inside my stomach, making my knees turn to rubber, and I grabbed onto the bar with both hands to steady myself. "Easy in there," I growled under my breath, aiming an angry glare towards the showboating guitar man that was Dominic as dipped and swayed like he was possessed. The crowd loved it, letting out a rousing roar of applause that scared the baby again. "Damn idiot," I lowered my hand to smooth over my belly, tapping my fingers against the booty bulge that tented my skin up, and the baby seemed to settle for the moment.

"You alright, Kat?" Kirby, my bartender and fellow packmate, paused just long enough to flash his steel blue gaze my way. He was short, not much taller than me, and nicely padded around the middle in the classic middle aged spread way. But his baby face and thick crop of short sheared mahogany hair had granted him that sweet trustworthy air that made you want to spill your guts to him. Plus, he was pretty good at talking people into buying drinks and food as they aired their problems too, and could make a damn good cocktail in about 15 seconds flat. When I didn't answer right away, he started

45

walking my way, his brows furrowed tightly in concern and hands still shaking his mixer.

"Fine, fine. The little one just got startled with the music and decided to kick my stomach into submission." I waved off his concern with a flick of my hand, but he still scowled.

"Are you sure? Maybe you need to go to the hospital and get checked?"

"Nope, I'm fine." I patted my belly with two hardy thumps. The heavy fabric of the black apron tied around my middle rippled as my baby answered back, stretching the flame orange sizzling flames logo into an oval shape. The sheer form fitting black lace top I was wearing didn't offer to hide any secrets either, and matched with my red pleather miniskirt and strappy black heels, there wasn't much room to hide anything. Whipping the apron over my head, the strands of dangling silver star earrings banged into my chin, and I tossed the apron under the bar. "I'm gonna run for a quick break, and I'll be right back."

"Okay," Before he could say anything else, a group of four drunk sorority girls were tipping dangerously close to falling over on the other side of the counter, and he rushed to serve them before they could grab another bottle of tequila. I chuckled softly to myself. God, I remember those days. It seemed so easy, worrying about nothing more than passing your next test and when you could meet up with your partner for a quick make out session before the bell rang. But I suppose life has a strange way of knocking you back on your ass and making you take a second look at yourself.

A sudden jab to my bladder served as a painful reminder of just how full it was, and I heaved a sigh and started waddling towards the kitchen when something snagged my arm. I spun, my head going a little weightless for a moment before a familiar set of eyes floated into my vision. "Hey there, beautiful." Ronan grinned, his thick lips pulling back to expose square white teeth starting to sharpen into fangs. "You shouldn't be working, it's bad stress on my baby. I want to make sure that we're having a healthy child together." He dropped his gaze to stare pointedly at my belly, and his tongue flicked out to lick his lips.

I froze, my heart thundering in my throat. Ronan was here? In the crowded bar with all of my pack members here? How did he do it? I hadn't even smelled him and my nose was super sensitive now. He shifted to lean across the bar, a strange medicinal scent rolling off his body, and that's when it hit me. He was taking scent suppressors, that's how they couldn't pick up his scent. "This isn't your baby, you ass! I can promise you that!" One wide palm started to grope for my belly, and I reached down the bar and grabbed the first thing that came to my fingertips. Cold stainless steel didn't really damage a werewolf any, but the smooth blade of the knife easily slipped between my fingers and I slammed it point first through his palm.

He growled low, gold eyes nearly bursting out of their sockets, and the crack of bones breaking made my stomach climb up in my throat to join my heart. There was a shout, but I didn't take time to listen. I grabbed a second knife and swung up, aiming a slice directly under his chin. Ronan pulled back, lunging into the crowd with wide eyes, and flared his nostrils. "You're right." He mumbled, his massive chest swelling with the breath. "Now I know why you left me. You have that damn gimp's child in your belly. He stole you from me."

"Shut your damn mouth!" It had to be the wolf in my veins giving me extra strength, because I planted my palms on the bar and swung my legs over. Moving faster than what I've felt in months, I brandished my knife at his throat and started backing him towards the mass of teaming bodies. "That's my business, not yours. We were through before I ever got pregnant." My eyes were burning, the words slipping out of my lips were turning into growls. My skin was crawling, aching to shift into the lush furry coat and the strong legs that could run for miles, but I kept it down just short of my bones breaking and rearranging themselves. "Why do you keep pestering me? Is it because that- ah!"

Like a red-hot iron band had just clamped around my stomach, I screeched and fell to my knees, my arms holding my belly like they could keep it intact. The muscles fluttered and twitched, stiffening as hard as stone, and the baby took that as encouragement to twist inside me. I tried to breath out slowly, but a second bolt made my lungs seize up. The floor beneath my feet spinning and a soft darkness started to creep in on the sides of my vision.

"Quick, we need to get her somewhere calm." A calm, authoritative voice cut through the dim clouds of my mind, and I felt myself being lifted and carried away from the dizzying blur of the screaming voices. A warm firm chest held me up where my spine slumped like it was goo, the familiar scent of warm skin and pine calming some of the churning in my stomach, and I slitted open one eye to see Tyler's granite hard jaw hovering inches away from my eyes. The tiny muscles twitched and flexed, stopping his teeth from grinding together, but also outlining the very obvious pulse drumming away in his neck.

"Tyler?" I murmured, still half dazed, but another bout of the pain crushed my belly and I muffled a scream into his shoulder.

"Try to relax, Kat." His voice was like steel, making room for no arguments whatsoever, and the wolf in me relaxed at the sound of her Alpha's authority, but the human half wanted to slap him.

"Where did he go?" I ground out through gritted teeth. My brow tightened, a slick coat of sweat clinging to the back of my neck, and pasted my shirt to my body. "I'm going to kill that asshole!"

"You'll have to get in line. When the pack saw you hop across the bar with a knife and then go down, there was no holding any of us back." He chuckled darkly, turning sideways to bump a door open with his hip. His aviators had slipped down his nose, exposing a glittering slice of dangerously dark eyes, and he flashed a wink my way. "I told Dom to save you a piece to gnaw on for later."

"Good." The air changed as he stepped inside, turning dryer and much cooler as the familiar musty scent of the storeroom greeted my nose. I let out a sigh of relief, relaxing slightly into his hold as the pain lessened and the baby rolled over, bumping the side of my belly against Tyler's chest.

"I see someone is telling me thanks for keeping their mama safe. So how about you two both take a good long rest here, I called for an ambulance and they should be here shortly to check you both out." Filled with boxes of liquor, food supplies, and the other assorted supplies that kept us running as a business from day to day, Tyler's stride slowed as he weaved through the storeroom, exploring more with the tips of his toes and squinting harder to see in the dim light. Shit, I've really got to get some more lightbulbs in this place.

"Tyler, to your right. There's a big wooden shipping crate that I received some imported scotch in, do you smell it?"

"Yeah." He turned, taking slow cautious steps towards the big chair sized box.

"Let me sit on it. I'm okay." Another tightening motion spread across my belly, starting from the top down and not stopping until it felt like my pussy was about to pop open. Scratch that, it felt like my entire belly was about to erupt like one of those science class volcanoes. If he could tell, he didn't say anything, nodding slowly and making his way to the crate until I could scoot myself out of his arms. The cool wood was slightly rough, cutting right through my miniskirt and brushing right against the heated skin of my thighs. I winched, keeping one hand on my belly for balance, and it tossed and wobbled with the baby deciding to practice some acrobatics while in mid contraction. The contrast of stretching and tightening of the muscles made me hiss out a curse under my breath, and Tyler dropped to his knees at my side like I'd kneed him in the crotch.

"Hey, you in there." Feeling around for a moment to get his bearings, he laid his face against my belly and growled low. "Take it easy on your momma. She was just trying to protect you, and you need to let her calm down for a moment before she can play with you again."

He glanced up at me for permission, and I murmured a small noise as he inched his fingers to my sides, pulling the sheer fabric of my shirt up to bear my belly to the air. Starting with slow strokes from the top down with just his fingertips, he started one of those massages that felt so good.

My belly visibly wobbled between us as he slid his hands down, fingers twisting in small itchy scratchy movements that felt heavenly against the too tight skin. Tyler beamed, feeling the happy movement as the baby enjoyed the massage and started to show its appreciation with a few hearty thumps. I moaned softly, arching my back just enough that the full weight of my belly rolled forward into his hands. It must be the sculptor's hands, because he knew exactly which tense spots to apply the lightest pressure, sending tingling shockwaves curling through the stretched nerves. As his hands slid lower, I felt the soft pressure as he pressed up, taking up some of the weight of my belly into his grasp

I winched, my entire body tensing in response to a quick breath. My belly shifted under his hands, the muscles tightening from the top and quickly spreading down like a wave, and the pressure of the baby pushed out against his left hand. "Kat," Tyler whispered low, his voice so deep that it sent chills down my spine.

"I'm fine." I insisted again even as my muscles shifted hard as a rock, squeezing so tight that I was sure I would pop. "It will pass, they always do." What normally passed was the little cramping pains, not the ones like these that had my teeth grinding together, but after what seemed like forever. It did finally let go, and it left me sweat soaked and gasping. Grabbing onto Tyler's shoulders for support, the distant song of the ambulance sirens sang out their ear clawing song as I screamed with another one, sure that I was about to pop open at any moment.

10

Tyler

"KAT, ARE YOU SURE YOU'RE okay?" Tucking my hands deep into the pockets of my jeans, I watched her blurry form shift in the shallow yellowish light, turning her pink hair a much darker shade and her arms folded around her belly.

"Was the opinion of the two ambulance workers not enough for you? I'm fine, it was just Braxton Hicks contractions." She snapped, and her glare shot daggers through my heart. "Now will you quit worrying. We are fine, I just want to run for a little while and burn off some of this energy."

After the unexpected arrival of the rogue, things settled down as Dom and a few pack members escorted Kat's ex into police custody for disturbing the peace and assaulting a pregnant woman. The ambulance checked Kat out, gave both her and the baby the all clear, and wanted to take her to the hospital but she refused. No amount of pleading, begging, and Alpha commands would sway her, and I couldn't stop worrying that something was wrong. Yes, her contractions had continued to grow weaker, but she was so close to being due that I couldn't stop worrying about her and the baby. And now she wanted to do something that had been totally off limits for months.

She wanted to run as a wolf.

"Kat, the stress of the change is normally not great for a pregnant werewolf. I can't remember any lady even trying it in our pack as far back as I can remember." Okay, that basically included my mom when she was pregnant with my brother, but still. Our bones shifted entirely, muscles stretching and lengthening to accompany the wolf's stride. It wasn't an easy process on the best of days, and took a lot of energy. Plus, what would even happen with the baby? All the room she needed for her womb would have to be put somewhere, and a furry four-legged body only had so much room.

With a huff and a sigh, she didn't wait to answer me. Instead, she used her body. The soft rasp of her clothes whipped away, and her bones cracked, the squishing squeaks of her organs shifting around sounded so much louder than mine did. Her milk scent grew heavier too, so sweet that I could barely stand it. The pale wash of yellow moonlight flooded her body, letting me see how her back hunched over and she shifted to all fours. The grass crunched beneath her feet as she flopped down on her side, her breathing so heavy like she had already run through the forest, and her skin tone changed. Becoming a mix of creamy white and streaked with silver and black. A whine pulled up out of my throat, my legs guiding me right to her side where I cautiously reached out towards her shoulder. She didn't say anything, just lying there with her massive swollen flank pulsing with every breath, and a pang of fear started to gnaw at my heart. Was she hurt? Had the change taken too much out of her?

"Kitty Kat?" I buried my fingers in her thick fur, my heart slamming double time in my chest. Her belly was so swollen in this form, even more than her human form. Like her entire midsection was about to burst, her skin felt hot and sore, stretched to the limit beneath her silky fur. I shouldn't have let her change. Pregnant werewolves couldn't handle this type of change at all. Stupid, stupid, stupid!

The shape shifted, vaguely raising her head, and the pointed ears shifted. I couldn't make out her eyes, but her jaw dipped down and the rough length of her hot tongue flicked out against my hand. With a deep rumbling groan, she heaved herself to her feet, swaying so badly that I thought she was going to tip over on her face. A growl of worry rumbles in my chest, and I try my best to swallow it down as she starts to stand.

With trembling legs like a baby fawn, Kat pulls herself to her feet and smashes her wolf muzzle into my face. At this close of a range, I can see the way her eyes are sparkling with mischief, and she flicks out her long pink tongue to swipe across my cheek before galloping off. Her stride was slightly uneven and much slower than I was used to hearing, but steadily thumped away into the forest.

Heaving out a sigh, I plopped down on the grass and pulled out my phone. A quick swipe of my finger across the screen had the little mechanical voice reading off all my messages, most of them were just junk that Dom had decided to fill up my phone with, but there were a few from the other members of the pack. One in particular was from Alex, the little computer nerd that handled all the pack's bills and trust distribution. He didn't say exactly what he needed, just that it was urgent. I frowned, staring down at the lit screen of my phone, and flicked down to his number.

"Call Alex?" The screen reader asked and I confirmed. What could have happened? Was someone trying to hack into the pack's bank account? Or had Dom overcharged his credit card again at the strip club? No matter how often it happened, usually things Dom related didn't require an urgent message.

"Alpha, thank you for calling me back so promptly." Ferociously frigid and so robotic that it was like I was talking to a computer, Alex's voice drifted down the line in his normal fashion, completely with all the clickety clack sounds of his keyboard. "There was a discrepancy involved with your latest charge at the Beautiful Dawn Maternity Care Center. One item in particular was listed as 'vitamins' on your receipt, but the pharmacy listed the item as Oral Scent Suppressors. Do you still want this charge processed?"

Scent Suppressors? What was Kat taking those for? Maybe so that her ex couldn't smell her and the baby, but that was before we knew he was outside. My hand started to wander towards my mouth, the edge of a fingernail slipping between my teeth, and I bit down before fully realizing what I was doing. No! Can't do that! Gotta stop that habit! "Yeah, sure. It's fine. Go ahead and process it, Alex." First, she was being so shady about the baby's father, and now I'd learned she was taking scent suppressors? What was up with Kat? I'll have to find her and ask her.

"As you wish, Alpha." The line died with a small click. No ifs, ands, or have a good day from him. Maybe I should check for a pulse sometime and make sure he wasn't a computer too. A small chuckle managed to worm its way out of the tightness in my chest, and I shoved the phone in my pocket, planting both of my palms against the soft grass to push myself up when something hit my back. Like a furry bowling ball charging into my spine, my legs crumbled and rolled beneath me, and I didn't stop until the ground crushed out a loud woosh from my lungs.

What the hell was that?

I blinked, trying to sort out the spinning haze of vaguely blue and green blurs above my head, and felt the tiny rivers of sensation struggling to return to my limbs. Fingers wriggled, back hurt but seemed okay, and anything below my waist was pinned by a very hot and heavy weight. Tilting my head up, I glanced down just in time to see the fur ball explode, every single scrap of hair retreating like someone was vacuuming up a carpet, and leaving behind perfectly pink, perfectly naked skin behind. Bones snapped and popped, so loud that it sounded like an anvil strike in my head, and the rest of Kat's features shifted into focus as the wolf retreated.

"Kat! What are you-" She leaned forward, sprawling her hands on either side of my shoulders and rested some of her weight back on her knees. Any words I had left died a quick death as she angled her knees on both sides of my hips, the smooth tautness of her belly pressed directly into my abs, and my fingers curled into the grass instead of trying to hold her body. "Kat," I tried to warn, but she's too far gone. Wolf gold still glowed in her eyes, but it was much darker. Hungrier almost, and damn it if it didn't send a pulse straight between my legs. Her delicate fingers danced closer to my skin, the grass crinkling like fresh paper between her fingers, and her heavy breasts swayed against my chest as she leaned down to place her lips against my ear.

"Wanna play?" She cooed playfully, her fingers inching down my sides, slowly pulling my shirt up in tiny bunches. It took a lot of strength I didn't know I had not to lean down and kiss that hell raising smirk off her face. I swallowed hard, my throat suddenly so dry that it felt like the sides were glued together, and I watched as her body tilted back and blurred as she whipped my shirt up to my neck. The press of her hot bare skin against mine is intoxicating, sending a rush straight up to my head, and my cock answers in kind as her breasts drag down my chest. Leaving behind a small trail of dampness where her nipples leaked, a small groan worked its way out of my chest as her lips trailed down my stomach, each touch scorching straight through my spine, and everything down below was suddenly way too tight.

'Where's this come from, Kitty Kat?" Not that I was complaining in the least, I know she had to feel my cock trying to rip out of my jeans, and my head fell back against the grass when she pressed her core against my thigh and grinded down. Fuck, she was wet. My hands left the grass and flew straight to her hips, keeping her there as her fingers started to tease apart my belt. The heavy chink of metal falls apart in her hands, and the sweet relief of pressure is replaced with something much hungrier. Her hand cups my cock, tracing every curve with her fingertips, and it throbs right in her hand. "Fuck, baby!" I cursed without thinking, and it only encouraged her.

"So sensitive, aren't you Tyler?" She teased, timing the swirl of her hand with a grind of her hips. My hand roams around the base of her spine, kneading in against the plush curve of her ass, and she moans when I squeeze tight in warning.

"Don't tease me. Not about this." I start to lean up, intending to capture her lips in a kiss, but she drops down and away. Her elbows spread wide, the mass of her belly dragging against the inside of my legs. Two hands prop up my hips, delicate fingers tracing over the curves of my hips and whipped my boxers down. Then she slides me to the hilt, the soft warmth of her mouth and the flat of her tongue flicking playfully around the swollen head.

Starting off slow, she uses a combination of her hands and her tongue to make me lose my mind. My hands curled in her hair, so desperate for something to hold on that it hurts, and my legs tremble against the grass. This wasn't what I wanted, but oh God did it feel good, and I cum faster than an overexcited teenage boy. A cloud drifts across the moon, cloaking everything in shadows, and what little I could make out of her face pales in comparison to the feel of her throat hugging my cock. Easily swallowing every ounce of my cum, and her tongue licks me clean before she breaks away with a soft pop of wet lips.

"Thanks, Tyler. I gotta go home now." A hazy flash of a smile sluggishly translates through my head, and I watch in stunned awe as she slowly eases to her feet, braces one hand against the swollen curve of her belly, and stumbles back into the forest. The wet slap of her thighs rubbing together echoes in my ears, but just barely due to my heart still pulsing in my ears, and the fierce burning in my chest vaguely reminds me to breathe somewhere normally. If it hadn't been for my softening cock laying against my thighs, still damp from the combination of her lips and my cum, and the sweet rush fogging my head, I wouldn't have believed something like this had happened.

It had to be a dream. Yeah, that's it. It had to be one just like the others, but then why did it feel so real?

I WOKE UP TO THE FEELING of something too large trying to rip its way out of my belly, the baby rolling over inside me to poke its butt directly into my spine. I sighed, my eyes flashed open to the ceiling, and a distinctive wetness started to make itself known against my thighs. Really? I was horny now? I supposed diving for Tyler after my run and trying to suck his cock off his body hadn't helped matters either. I groaned, slapping a hand against my forehead. Why did I let the full moon energy get to me like that?

A soft knock at the door pulled me out of my head and back into the now, Sandy's baby soft whisper barely trickling through the door. "Kat, are you okay? I was just checking before I have to go to work."

"Yeah, yeah. 'M fine." Great, now I had her worried too. I rolled myself out of bed like a lumbering walrus and stumbled to the door, kept slightly off balance by my wriggling passenger inside. Sandy was waiting just on the other side, nervously shifting from foot to foot, and tugged at the tight fabric of her uniform across her breasts. "What?" I snarled, slightly sharper than I meant to, and she skittered back like a frightened fawn.

"N-Nothing! I just wanted to make sure that you were okay before I left." It was almost an exact same repeat of what she said before, and the way her heart was pounding, I couldn't tell if it was me or something else that had her so nervous. Curling her shoulders over like her spine was bending double, she followed me into the kitchen where I started to grab a drink of water when someone knocked at the door.

"Morning, Kitty Kat." Someone growled on the other side of the door, just low enough that I could hear it, but Sandy couldn't. My arm froze in midair, still reaching for the glass on the shelf, and my eyes widened. Oh, hell no!

"Excuse me," Brushing past Sandy, and probably scaring a few years off her life, I stomped to the door and opened it with a single push. Standing there in a small halo of fuzzy yellow light from the fluorescent lights above was Tyler in his morning best. Unfortunately for me, that meant his short hair still artfully tousled from sleep, a coating of dark stubble covering the lines of his jaw, and a beautiful perky smile that made my heart stumble in my chest like a toddler trying to walk.

My hand tightened on the door, a familiar ache started to bloom between my thighs, and I sucked in an unsteady breath. "Morning, Kat!" He murmured, his deep voice made even huskier by the hazy edge of sleep still clinging to the edges, and I struggled not to rub my thighs together just to get a little relief. I wonder what he sounded like if- No! Bad thought train!

"Hell, no! I don't need a fucking babysitter!" I don't care how hard my heart slammed against my chest, I started to slam the door in his face. He blocked it, bracing his thick left arm over my head and pushed it firmly back against the wall.

"I'm not a babysitter. Sandy has to work, you need to rest, I need your input on something, and someone needs to make sure that you don't pop out into full labor alone." He dropped his eyes to something at his feet, and mine followed like they were magnetized. A small item was bundled in a protective gray cloth, strangely lumpish, and it seemed familiar somehow. "Plus," He dropped his voice lower, curling over to let his chin hover above my shoulder. "I *really* want to talk to you about last night."

My eyes stretched wide, the smell of his freshly washed skin jogging the memories of last night in the trees. The tall oaks and the soft grass beneath my bare feet. Him, laying spread out on the grass like my own fucking buffet, and the way he curled his hands in my hair when I lapped my tongue around his cock. Damn, if I hadn't needed a reason to change my underwear before, I did now.

"Do what you want. I got to change." He didn't need to ask why, his nostrils flared. Taking in my scent for himself, and a barely audible growl rumbled through his chest. A dark hunger glowed in his eyes, the beginning strands of wolf gold threading around the swollen inky pupil, and his smile widened as he watched me step back.

"Are you sure that you are going to be okay?" Sandy blinked her big eyes my way, and I forced myself to focus on her and not the way Tyler prowled forward to take a seat on my couch.

"Yeah, fine." It came out breathless, distracted, and I shoved my hand through my hair and rumpled the strands into even sharper spikes. She hesitated, nervously pawing at her purse strap and gnawing on her lower lip, but finally nodded her head and left. The click of the door felt like a gunshot, the air thickening with tension and it was making my head swim. For a lack of anything better to do, I waddled to my room and dug out another pair of dry underwear. My laundry bill was going to be seriously high if he didn't leave soon, either that or I would explode.

"Hey, you wanna watch a movie or something too?" Tyler called out from the couch, and I huffed. Leaning back against my bed and trying to reach around my belly to pull my underwear down was now an Olympic sport, and then- crap! There's another one. I winched as my belly stiffened with a small contraction, but I managed to snag the little scrap of fabric with one finger and pulled it down. It came away with a soft snap, the elastic and wet fabric pooling on the floor like some kind of limp white alien, and I kicked it into the laundry basket with my toe.

"Whatever!" I was about to pull my replacement pair of underwear on when a nasty little thought tickled my brain. If he insisted on staying, then I should be comfortable right? That's what he wanted me to do, be comfortable, and there wasn't much more comfortable than what clothes I was thinking of. Flinging my underwear back into the drawer, I waddled to the closet and pulled out a favorite of mine. A black mesh number that tied with a little ribbon just under my breasts, and then flared out in a v across my belly. The open sides fell like wings against my ribs, brushing the tops of my hips with the lace edge, and the cups still just held my breasts. It was a breeze to slip on, one of the few things that still was, and I padded out into the den with a seductive smile on my face. "Hope you don't mind that I slipped into something more comfortable." I purred, adjusting my glasses to watch his face as it slowly turned from the screen to me.

At first, he didn't respond, his jaw going slack and his eyes glassy as I sank down onto the couch beside him with a heavy groan. Rocking back as far as the support of the sofa would allow, the twinges and aches in my spine started to release as something else beside me decided to hold up my belly. Which also meant that the full roundness of my belly spilled out into my lap, twitching heavily as the baby started to wake up and decided it was party time.

"So, what are we watching?" Circling my thumbs against a track of red that snaked up my sides, I glanced out of the corner of my eye to see that he had lost all interest in the movie, but was instead focusing on me. Tight focus lines surrounded his eyes, pulling them tight as he squinted, trying to focus his wandering eyes as they traced every inch of my body from head to toe. I smiled, feeling a little proud of myself at the moment. "Something wrong?" I pointedly stare at the sudden rise of his pants in the junction of his thighs. Even if he couldn't see me clearly, I know he could feel the way I was looking at him.

"Oh, yeah." He murmurs, but it's hazy like an afterthought. Tyler curls back up into the couch, holding one pillow over his lab, and shifts as far away as the sofa will allow. God, it's like he's trying to mold himself to the arm, half of his upper body perched on top like some sort of freaky cat. A snort leaks out of my throat, and maybe I should give him a little mercy. Shifting my focus over to the tv, I take up the role of the description reader and start telling him all the important parts he should know. Luckily it's an action movie we've both seen a thousand times and it doesn't require a whole lot of thought.

The entire time I'm talking, someone else decided to have their share of the conversation. My skin rolls and shivers, shaken out of place by the baby's movements as it shifts its weight from left to right. Sometimes the entire mass of my belly draped over my right hip, like it was trying to reach over and touch Tyler. Mixing in several hops that made my belly bounce up and down like it was filled with jumping beans, and I couldn't help but groan each time the pair of feet made contact with my spine.

"Does that hurt?" He asked ever so innocently as I groaned and arched my back, trying to make a little more room as the baby shoved its feet down towards my crotch and rammed it's back into my lungs.

"Yeah!" The word rushed out in a woosh, and that was about all I had room for. Tilting into my hands, the baby lowered itself just enough that I could catch my breath before dropping down parallel to my spine and pushing out. A triangle shaped bulge formed in the top of my belly, pushed out by tiny hands that were trying to rip me apart. I swallowed a curse, winching as I draped my hands across my bare belly. This was a good thing. A very active baby was a healthy thing, as long as it didn't rip me apart!

"You mind if I try something?" I nodded, barely giving him space to answer, and the sofa squeaked softly as he laid down on his stomach. He wrapped his arms around my back, snuggling his face up against the side of my belly, and the scratchy sensation of his stubble made me snort. Small circles started to form in the dimples of my hips, traced there by his thumbs. Like little fairy kisses, he starts peppering my belly with sweet pecks, one after another calmly climbing up and over the mountain of my belly, and it feels wonderful. Plus, it was having a great effect on the baby. The rib shaking kicks and squirms were slowing down, but the twitches of contractions were still crawling through my muscles. He must have picked up on it, moving his hands to brace himself on either side of my belly, and he swung his legs onto the floor.

My breath caught as he neatly slid down between my legs, his warm palms slowly spreading my thighs open and inserting his body between them. The cool air hits my lips like a bullet, everything bared to the light, and I suddenly started to wonder if this was a bad idea. If he could fully see everything, there's no telling what he'd think about seeing me already soaking wet, and all he's done is kiss my belly. Slowly, cautiously sliding his hands lower, he trailed one finger along the length of my mound all the way down, a low growl that's so deep it sounds feral rumbles out of his chest. "So damn wet. Is all this for me?"

Oh, shit! I'm fucked.

"Maybe." My hips started to squirm, eager for the stimulation those fingers promised that are just so close but yet so far. He pressed kiss after kiss to my belly, his finger slowly dipping down to drag over my clit, and smiling each time a twitch of movement pushed back. Opening his eyes, I struggled not to gasp at the pure hunger glowing in the depths, and I softly patted the back of his neck as he climbed higher. Following the pattern of stretch marks up to the top, his tongue licked a wet ribbon into each dip and curve of my skin, sometimes stopping to swirl his tongue in the junction where two scars merged as one. My head fell back on my shoulders, no longer able to meet his gaze, but I could feel every one of his hot breaths as they showered across my skin.

Heat blasts through my veins like an inferno, and my hips squirm against his weight pinning me down. Desperate for the contact that would satisfy the ache in my core, and I wined in frustration. A warm chuckle buried itself in the sensitive skin between my belly and my breasts, his stubble grazing thousands of tiny pinpricks against my skin, and it only stoked the ache higher. His tongue swirls out, leaving a trail that makes me keen like I'm broken, and my hand curls against the back of his neck. His hair is soft, so soft and silky. Just like the slight dark fuzz covering his chest and arms, and the fur of his wolf form.

A contraction started to twitch below my navel as he dipped down, teasingly brushing his lips across my own lower ones, and the soft caress of his breath against my clit has me on the verge of pleading for him to just get on with it already. I tried to shift again, my hips eagerly bucking up, and before I could speak, he slipped a finger inside me. The stretch doesn't even burn, I'm too slick for that. "So tight too." He murmurs softly, his lips leaving small bites along the sensitive inner skin of my thighs, and a second finger quickly joins the first. This slow, steady pumping stokes the heat in my belly, and I throw a hand across my mouth to muffle a shriek of frustration.

"F-Faster!" I tried to say, or at least I think I did. The air was thick and strong, musky with the scent of sex and the promise of even more to come. Riding on a sudden idea burst, I snaked my arms up and flipped the shirt over my head. The girls rolled free without hesitation, swaying in time with my body as he added a third finger inside.

A soft sigh leaks out of my lips as the pressure binding them decreases, but the cool air bites at the sensitive tip of my nipples, tightening the tips so hard that they ache in time with the pulse in my core. "Your heart's pounding." He murmurs idly, leaning up to mouth at my left nipple. It feels like a lightning bolt rams through my chest, his tongue casually flicking in time with the pumping of his fingers, alternating in a few gentle sucks and I can feel some of the pressure releasing as milk stains his lips. Threading my hand through his hair and pulling gently, it encouraged him into doubling the strength of his licks. His nimble tongue easily swirled around the puckered tips as he switched from one to another with a quick wet pop. More milk trickled down my chest, pooling in the crease of my belly, and flowed down my sides in warm tiny rivers.

Anything else I wanted to say is snatched away as the rhythm of his fingers increases, my hips matching his fingers thrust for thrust, greedily taking everything he was giving and begging for more. Just to add another layer of torture, his hips grinded against my leg, the tough fabric of his jeans not hiding any inch of his hard cock at all. His thumb circles my clit, adding just the right amount of pressure that has me seeing stars, and he sucks hard on my nipple. So hard that his cheeks hollow, and my breath catches in my chest. The cumming takes me by surprise, pulling me into a sea of ecstasy that floods my limbs with heat. For a moment, there's no pain. None at all, and I'm light as a feather.

Unfortunately, the high doesn't last forever. The intense cramping pain of my belly hardening once again brings me down, and my smile crumples into a scowl. His warm hands stopped, leaving my skin empty and cold. A rousing thump from inside echoes the squeeze, making my eyes water and my knees try to draw up towards my chest. "Shit!" I hissed out, drawing my lower lip between my teeth until I tasted blood on my tongue. Why were they so bad?

"Hey, easy." Tyler's soft voice drifted into my ear, and I felt the sofa dip as he sat back down. "Let's try this too." Blinking open my eyes, I didn't get what he meant, but my eyes hazily focused on something in his hands. A tall bottle with a squirt top, it took a moment for my foggy brain to catch up with the fact that he was holding my bottle of oil, and he slowly raised it right over my belly to- fuck!

The oil was cold and slick, easily sliding over my skin as he squirted a stream directly onto the top of my massive belly. I swore, my lips curling in a snarl, and his chuckle made my stomach jiggle with butterflies instead of pain. Well, shit. Now he's giving me butterflies and all that kind of crap. In sharp contrast to the smooth oil was the roughness of his hands, the thick calluses from years of working with his carving tools easily spread the smooth liquid around until my skin was shiny and perfect. The tightness eased some, the trembling muscles still twitching with the aftershocks of my orgasm. Or maybe it was another contraction? Either way, it worked. I leaned back with a sigh, idly rubbing my hand over the thick muscles of his thigh, and squeezed it slightly.

"You're so good at this. I wonder what else you're good at?"

His smile flashed; all wolf white teeth pulled up into a seductive grin. "Do you really want to know?"

12

Tyler

SHE LEANED BACK WITH a soft grunt, her belly sloshing lightly with the baby's movements, and I smoothed my hand across her knee. Her breath shook slightly, a shiver of goosebumps rising across her skin, and a small chuckle rumbled out of my chest. "And if I did, would that be a problem?" She said, and I could hear the self-satisfied smirk in her voice.

"Nope. Feel free to play as much as you want, Kitty Kat." Taking in a deep breath, the musky scent of her arousal hit me full force again, my stomach tightening on reflex just to try and keep me from cumming apart in my pants. Shifting back on my knees, I laid my cheek against her thigh and rested my palm against her lips. An insistent buck of her hips demanded my touch lower, my fingers easily sliding into the knuckle, and I grazed my finger lightly against the swollen bud of her clit. She moaned, all husky and deep, and the sound traveled straight to my cock. "Fuck, you're perfect! Taking my fingers so well. Makes me wonder how well you would take my cock."

She tries to say something, but it dies on her tongue when I lean up to her chest again. Pursing my lips, I sucked on the delicate skin of her right breast just lightly enough to feel but not to hurt, and feathered my tongue against the peak of her nipple. She moaned again, her fingers tightening like she was ready to rip out my hair by the roots as more of her creamy milk flooded my mouth. It was sweet, almost like coconut milk, but a little thinner.

"Oh, god!" Her voice changed, like it was partially muffled by a pillow. "More, *please.*"

A chuckle brewed low in my chest as I slid my hands up, cupping the full weight of her overfull belly in my hands. I've never heard Kat beg before, but damn if it wasn't intoxicating. My cock ached,

65

pulsing against the sheets trapped between it and the bed, and the slight dampness of cum was already sticking to my belly, smearing even more each time I twisted around. Her legs started to tremble against my hips, warning me of the orgasm about to burst free, and that was just what I needed to know. Hollowing my cheeks in for one last good suck, I let go of her nipple and slid down, spreading her folds with my fingers for the first lick.

Her back arched up, nearly bumping my face with her belly, and I smirked into the kiss as my tongue worked on her clit. She was so sensitive, the rapid pump of my fingers sliding in and out of her slick folds made these cute little wet snaps, and I curled my fingers up to stroke that special little spot. Her trembling increased, her hands nearly ripping my hair out as she tried to both push and pull me away from her lips. She was almost there, but not quite yet.

Pulling back, she whined at the loss of stimulation, her hips jolting up to meet my fingers, but I glanced up in the direction of her eyes. "Kitty Kat, you want to ride me? It should feel better to your back instead of lying there." My cheeks burn with a flush despite saying the words out aloud. Did I insult her?

"You're pretty good with this, aren't you?" The hand in my hair tugs questionably, pulling my head back up just a little, and a slight impression of something moving against the darkness caught my eye. She didn't answer, but slid her hands down my neck, flowing over my chest with just the faintest tickle over my nipples. My breath caught, a ripple rolling down my throat as I swallowed heavily. God, she was a tease. Everywhere her fingers touched tingled, the fabric of my shirt and my jeans couldn't hide it in the least, and they all traveled straight towards my cock.

"You said that I was wet for you, but what about you? Are you really this hard for little ole me?" Her fingers dipped down, briefly playing with the waistband of my jeans before diving beneath. My hands fisted against the couch, her fingers circling the head of my cock through my boxers. Ho-ly shit! And that was just her touch. Shaking my jeans off in record time, the warmth of her hand lazily pumping up and down has me hard *and* leaking in a few passes. My head falls back on my shoulders, too weak to stand straight anymore, and she does two more passes before adding a twisting thing that makes me want to burst right there. "You're so pretty when you moan though," The sofa creaks as she leans up as much as her belly will allow, the heat of her body smothering all thought from my head. She feels good, so good that it hurts.

Digging my palms into the sofa for purchase, I hauled myself up to sit beside her. Her hands cupped my face, thumbs tracing the lines of my cheeks, and I blinked as a sudden tightening in my chest threatened to overwhelm me. "Kat," What was I trying to say? What did I even want to say? The thought left as she climbed on top of me, the warmth and weight of her body causing too much friction, and she rocked her heated core against my lap. With just the thin scrap of my boxers separating us, my hips pushed up against her lips, and she flared one hand against my belly.

"Down, boy." She chuckled, the lumps and bumps of the baby shifted against my abs, and my fingers chased each movement until it slowed to a peaceful rest. Now only broken by the occasional twitches of her contractions, having her positioned this way let me rest my head right against her milk-stained chest. My ear pressed against her thudding heart and I closed my eyes, letting the soft patter of the baby's heartbeat combined with the authoritative pound of her own. "You're certainly excited. Wonder how long it would take before you're cumming inside me?" The little torturer grinds her lips against my thigh, spreading the sticky remains of her dampness across my leg, and trapped my cock along the underside of her belly. My hands flew to her hips for support, every nerve firing wildfire sparks, and it gave me an idea. I just hope that it doesn't backfire on me.

"Kat, do you trust me?" I gritted out through tightly clenched teeth.

She braced her hands against my chest, palms flat for maximum support, and I squeezed her hips to remind her to speak. "Yes." Was all she had to say, and that was all I needed. Her head tossed back against her shoulders as I looped my arms around her waist and hips, a soft squeak of surprise muffling itself into my neck. Tantalizingly soft puffs of breath raked against my skin, burning it even hotter than it was before. The sofa creaked, the rustling fabric shifting and crinkling beneath our weight as I stood up and retraced the memory of my steps to her room. Two delicate legs hooked around my hips, her toes pressed so tightly against my spine that they curled, and the muscles twitched under my touch as we both realized just exactly where this was going.

I DON'T KNOW WHETHER to laugh or sigh when his chest rumbles with a laugh, each slow and steady step perfectly measured to bring him to my bedroom door. So, I settled for pressing my lips against his throat. His breath hitched, a sway sneaking into his stride, and I smiled and pressed my body even tighter against him. Almost curved over like the letter c, my belly pressed so far into his abs that every shift of his body is plainly obvious, including the excited throb of his cock trapped against my core.

Pausing in the doorway, he tipped his head to the side and squinted. The brilliant light of his eyes shifting into tiny little slits that nearly disappear into his cheeks. "Five steps?" It's a strange question, one that crawls out of his throat like the words are being bitten out, but a delayed spark reminds me what he's asking. How much farther to the bed.

"For you, about six." Tyler swallows heavily, bobbing his head slightly before striding forward. Like I was made of glass, he carefully lowered me down onto the bed, and I wriggled around until my preferred pillows were positioned behind my back, shoulders, and neck. The bed dipped as he sat down, and the way the soft light slanted in through the door let me see some of my handiwork in real life. Blushed blood red from cheek to chest, the reddish blooms of my kisses speckled his skin like these cute little rose blooms. His eyes were fixed firmly on mine, a dark hunger deepening the shadows of his face, and every breath shook his entire body.

"You sure?" My legs tightened around his hips for my answer, pulling him down within perfect kissing range. Two hands brace themselves against the bed, keeping most of his weight off me, and give me the perfect advantage of exploring the firm muscles of his back with my fingertips. They clench and shiver, his hips joining mine in a rhythm perfect for fucking.

"What about you? You think you're up to the challenge?" I pop back, raking my nails down his sides as small red trails start blooming across his skin. He smirks, shifting to one side enough that he could drag his sensitive fingertips along the underside of my breasts. The rough edge of his thumb drew soothing circles around the outer rim of my nipple, making my rhythm studder for a few moments. It takes everything I have not to groan at the pressure in my chest begging to be freed, wanting to feel exactly what his hands can do. Just like before, he slowly starts to drop his head, the rough edge of his stubbled chin dragging against the upper curve of my belly, and my legs squirm against the dip in his spine. "You like that?" Hell yes! If it was possible, my nipples harden even more, like little pebbles rolling under his touch and he knows it. Pushing my heels against the base of his spine, I give him a little prod of encouragement to get things moving.

Kicking off his boxers with record speed, I propped a couple more pillows under my neck and watched as he slowly started to pump himself up with one hand. Already hard, the flushed crown of his cock matches his skin, both a deep red so bright that it almost looks painful. A thin trail of precum slides from the tip, glistening between his fingers with each smooth stroke. My mouth waters as my eyes wander up, all firm tanned skin lightly scored with deep scars, and his muscles flex and twist like living marble with every movement. He's beautiful, and deadly. A true Alpha made flesh, and my inner wolf perks up like someone is holding a steak in front of her nose.

"Like what you see?" He smirks, sauntering back over to the side of my bed with an extra sway to his hips. His empty hand fists against his swollen cock, leisurely traveling up and down like we had all the time in the world. My hand drifts between my legs, a finger neatly sliding between my lips. Fuck, I'm so wet. The slick comes even more as my thumb grazes my clit, his nostrils flaring in response. A solid thump echoes off the floor as he drops to his knees, his thighs tensing as his strokes grow faster, and he delicately peppers the inner skin of my thighs with his lips. "You smell so good." The soft growl vibrated straight through my skin, curling around my core, and I swear I could feel myself leaking just from his voice alone.

"H-hah! You can't honestly tell me pregnant pussy smells better than regular pussy." The words left my mouth in a whimper, those trailing lips drawing closer and closer to where I needed him most, but still not close enough. Even after coming twice before, my hips bucked up, too impatient to wait much longer, but Tyler chuckled and placed his hand flat against the curve of my underbelly. The warmth and weight of his touch felt wonderful, but it was so close to my needy crotch that I couldn't think. A small whimper, a buck of my hips, and I felt him smile as his hand slowly started to slide down.

"Your scent, all of it, has been driving me crazy for months. Why do you think Dom keeps giving me hell because I'm hard all the time?" My hands curled in his hair as his long fingers slid through my folds, gently exploring around for a moment before finding my swollen clit. Just like before, Tyler started with lazy touches that lingering around, but still not quite right. I couldn't see him, my belly was way too big, but I could feel the hot length of his tongue slowly drag against my lips. It made me want to scream, but all that could come out was a long moan. It felt so *good*. It stroked slowly, two fingers and then three circling around the inner edge of my lips but still not driving deep enough, and combined with the pressure of his thumb. It nearly drove me *insane* from want. All I'd tasted before was his fingers, now I wanted his cock too.

My lips were moving, chanting something like a prayer, and a vague version of his name penetrated my foggy brain as his tongue lapped at my core like he intended to drink me dry. Every drip of my slick, every inch of my core, swirling touches and gentle laps, everything he had, he gave out to me. Even when my hands tightened in his air, it spurred him on double, burying snarl after snarl in my core until I felt like I would break.

With a sharp snap, the ache in my core poured free. My muscles locked up, my head rolling back against the pillow, and his name screeching past my lips. Then it's bliss, my core shivering around the length of his fingers, but deep inside I still wanted more. When the hazy fog started to clear, I felt Tyler pull back, his wet cheek resting against my belly, and his dark eyes were wandering just above my head. "Sounds like you both enjoyed that." He smirked; the dark purr combined with those plump lips still shining with my slick instantly reignited the empty hunger in my core.

"Come here!" I curled my fingers in his hair, tugging sharply, and his eyes fluttered with a barely suppressed moan slipping out of his lips. Ooo, interesting. I pulled again, anticipation making little shivers running across my skin, and his eyes flash open to show off the dark iris stained with wolf gold. He slid forward, his heavy cock dragging against my thighs, and pressed his mouth to mine. I scowled, the bitter taste of my slick still clinging to his lips, but thrusted my tongue forward between his lips.

The deeper each kiss went, the more I tried to push my body against his. His muscular curves easily conforming around the awkward bulge of my belly, his cock pressing right up against my hips as his knee keeps my thighs spread apart. His head tips to one side, a silent question in his eyes, and I tugged softly at the tips of his hair. "'S okay." My thick tongue mumbles, and the pink tip of his tongue licks the lower edge of his lip as he slowly nods.

A shiver quivered through my insides as his right hand cups around his cock, the broad tip leaking a small drop of pearly fluid, and uses his left hand to guide my leg up around his hip. He slides in easily with a soft squelch, slowly inching forward with each breath like he was afraid I would break. It's taking all his control, his nostrils flaring with each deep breath, and a tight wrinkle formed between his eyes. There's no way he could hurt me, not now, and I pushed my heel against his hip to spur him on. Tyler snapped forward, sliding fully in with a single thrust, and my breath rushed out of my lungs in one quick hiss.

"Ohmygod! Are you okay! Did I hurt you?" His large hands fluttered over my body, a safety check just in case any of my parts broke off, and normally I would have appreciated it. Loved it so much that I could have kissed his lips off, but not when my core was aching for him to get on with it.

"I'm fine." Wrapping my arms around his neck, I pulled myself up as far as I could and smothered his lips in a formless kiss. Anything else he was trying to say was smothered out with a groan, his tongue sweeping forward to tangle with mine, and one thick arm braced itself against my back. Pressed so tightly against him that I could feel his heart racing against my chest, Tyler buried his face between my neck and shoulder and twisted. Pulling me on top of him as he flopped onto his back, the full impact of this position didn't hit until I slid down. My weight combined with gravity pushed his cock at just the right angle to stroke that spot, the one that made me see stars again, and my hands flew to his chest for support.

"You seemed to like this before. So, let's try it again." His voice rumbled through his chest and straight into my hands, the damp sheen of sweat adding an extra glow to his flushed skin. With firm muscles rippling like water under my hands, he leaned up and swirled his tongue against my nipples, pressing a soft kiss to each tip and blinking those dark golden eyes up at me. "Plus, there's a whole new angle to explore that I really like." A thrust up confirmed his point, ripping a groan out of my throat and lighting a fire in my blood.

Using what strength I had left in my legs, I started to grind and ride him as hard as I dared. The wolf in my veins howled out her pleasure each time his kiss swollen lips pressed to my heavy chest, sucking lightly from my bouncing breasts while one hand splayed against the small of my back. Keeping me grounded but also kneading into the sore spots, his hand felt like magic and the other kneaded the skin of my hip. "Fuck it! You feel so good!" My fingers tunneled through his dark hair, creating a tousled mess out of the short strands, and his eyes brightened with encouragement.

"You like my cock like this?" Tyler smiled, a small trace of white milk staining his lips. Through the haze of bliss, I noticed there was something else a little naughty twisting his lips higher. "Then, how about you come for me?"

Blurring with wolf speed, he snaked a hand between our bodies when I raised up, pushing his fingers against my clit when I dropped down, and I screamed out. His stroking fingers added just that extra push I needed to my clit, combined with his lips as he sucked a ring of kisses around my neck. Starting slower, like a fire first starting to build, then burning higher and faster, his hips bucked up to meet my thrusts with a frantic pace. I was close, so close that I couldn't breathe.

Then I felt his teeth, his wolf fangs, plunge into the meat of my shoulder.

I came with a garbled cry of his name, sweet relief flooding through my veins, and my core clutches his cock so hard that I feel him stiffen. His thrusts stutter, a warm wet heat flooding my insides, and then he fell backwards, pulling me with him. I twisted sideways, landing on my left hip with my right leg still stretched across his hips. A small empty ache started to knead at my core when his softening cock slipped out, but it was quickly swept away by his warm hands roaming over my ribs. He didn't even seem to mind the weight of my belly pressed against his stomach; the baby suspiciously quiet for now.

We laid there tangled together until we both started to breathe normally. My ear laid against his chest, his rapid heartbeat gradually slowing down to a more relaxed pace, and the rasp of air moving through his lungs was so soothing that my eyes started to close. The nagging thoughts that I needed to get up and clean up could wait, especially when his fingers started trailing through the strands of my hair with long strokes. I sighed, nuzzling my cheek against Tyler's chest, and listened to the beginning notes of a raspy hum start to take shape in his throat.

14

Tyler

My eyes flew open, the tinkling sound felt like tiny mice in stilettos were clog dancing in my ears. The hell? Where did that come from?

Rolling over onto my stomach, I folded the pillow under my neck and blinked slowly. It came again, this time even louder, and the sound of a name being shouted at me finally pierced through my head. "Dom! Dom!" The electronic voice squealed like a computerized fangirl, and I ruffled a hand around the base of my neck before reaching over and slapping the phone on.

"Someone better be dying for you to wake me up like that."

"For someone who just spent all yesterday and last night getting laid, you're in an awfully sour mood." Dom chuckled on the other end of the line, but it lacked some of his usual vigor. Underneath his voice, I could hear a lot of voices all mixed together in a frantic chatter. The kind of chatter that makes your hair stand up from sheer panic. Before I could get my tongue working, he stepped away into a much quieter area. "Listen, bro. I'd love to tease you about this, but we've got big problems. Kat's crazy ex escaped sometime last night. Pulled the iron bars out of the damn wall of his cell. The sheriff almost had a heart attack from shock, and his deputy is a quivering mess that's still hiding under his desk."

"When?" I snapped back, tucking my phone between my chin and shoulder as I swung my legs over the side of the bed. How had he even broken out of the county jail? We had wolves around the outside too. Trying to think of all the possibilities made my head throb, so I settled on the one thing I could control right now. Finding my pants.

"This morning, about 2 a.m. He snuck out between patrols, and ran for the woods outside of down. He must have had a stash of scent killers hidden somewhere, because we could pick up his trail so far and then it just vanished. Poof!" The clap of his hands smacking together punctuated the idea, and my lips parted in an o of surprise when my hands flattened against the bed and a piece of sturdy fabric met them. My jeans. Kat must have folded them up and placed them beside me.

"I'll get Kat and bring her to the meadow. The rogue will most likely be searching for her." Hooking my fingers in the loops of my jeans, a swift tug brought them up. Now that I was awake, the extra rattling sounds seemed to be coming from the shower. Good, Kat was fine. I'd love to talk to her about last night, but it would have to wait. "Keep me posted on any updates."

"You betcha!" With a chirp and a click, the line went dead, and I placed my phone back on the table. Something smooth and round brushed my hand, rattling slightly as it bounced off the table and rolled away, and I scowled into the darkness. I really needed some more light in here. My jeans crinkled as they folded around my knees, a small ache in my back making itself known as I bent over and started running my hands in large sweeps across the floor. Luckily the bottle hadn't rolled too far, and I had started to pick it up when my ears caught something new. The wet slap-slap of bare feet padding across the floor.

"What the hell are you doing?" Frigid cold and totally bitch level angry, Kat's body was briefly outlined by the light from the bathroom, making things a tiny bit brighter than they normally were. Bright enough that I could see the pink fuzz on top of her head, and that her arms were crossed over her breasts. There wasn't a towel in sight, her beautiful bare body standing there as naked as the day she was born, and my cock suddenly decided that morning wood felt really good right now. "Why are you prowling through my stuff?"

"Easy!" My hands flashed up against my chest, showing her my empty palms. "It fell off and I was picking it up."

It didn't satisfy her, her bare feet slapping against the floor as she stomped forward and bent down. The urge to help her hit me like a fist, especially from the extra groans and grunts she let out, but I was halfway afraid to in case it irritated her further. With tiny shuffled steps, I inched back on my knees towards the bed. Funny how that felt like safety right now. "You shouldn't have been nosing in my stuff. It's mine!" She threw out each word like it was a weapon.

"It's just your vitamins, isn't it? It wasn't really anything that hurts or is pretty fragile, right?" She didn't answer, a deadly silence like those moments in the movies before the serial killer popped out of the shadows came down. I swallow slowly, grabbing onto the bed with both hands and heaving myself backwards. Yes, more distance needed. My wolf seemed to encourage this, that and rolling over and showing her my belly. It felt plastic, and rattled like a pill bottle. So, I was assuming that it was her vitamins, but what if it wasn't? Crap, I hope I didn't just break something really expensive. "It was just your vitamins, right?"

"What it was is none of your business!" Her snarl could have peeled the paint from the walls. She stalked over to a corner of her room and flipped the light on. Bright white light suddenly flooded the room, and it took a moment for my eyes to adjust. Her pink hair and the blur of her body soared into view, one short leg stuck out and angrily tapping a foot against the ground. Her focus had shifted away, down to the bottle fumbling around in her hands, and I let out a tiny breath of relief at that. With a quick flick, the cap popped off, bouncing across the floor to land at my feet, and a wave of scent hit me like a gunshot.

Scent Suppressors. That musty, slightly chalky smell was unforgettable, especially considering that I had just smelled it before on the rogue. Confusion scratched at my mind, curling down through my thoughts as several events lined up in my head. The mysterious vitamins from the clinic, the different charges, why her own scent was never very loud. "Kat," I started slowly, my tongue still refusing to work properly. "Why are you taking scent suppressors? The baby's father, he's not that guy in your story, is he?"

"Yes, he is! Why would I make up something like that?"

"I don't know. Because you won't tell me the truth about anything? Ever since you came back to town, you won't share anything about the baby or you. So how do I know that what you said was true, and that the baby isn't from that wackjob that's out running around?"

"Because the baby is yours! It's always been yours!" She cried out, her voice quavering with a sob that I couldn't see. Tossing the bottle aside, the pills rattled as they hit the floor, eerily imitating what my heart was doing in my chest. Both of her arms folded around her belly, like she was protecting it from the world, and the slightest tremble shook her shoulders. Ice water ran through my veins, delivering a crushing blow to my gut like the worst sucker punch I've ever felt.

The baby was mine. But how? There's never been anything between us except my wet dreams, right?

"About nine months ago, when I came back for a visit during the winter and you were fucked over by that cold. That's when it happened. I didn't think you'd remember, or that any of this-" Her hand blurred as she waved it over her belly, "-would happen. Mother Nature sure had a different way of saying you're screwed." A raspy chuckle leaked from her throat, but it was so hollow that I could have reached right through it.

Mine. Kat. The baby. It was all mine. It didn't seem real. My knees turned gummy, twisted out from under my body, and I sank back down on the bed. All the way back then, I thought I was just delirious from the fever, but that had actually happened? A tightening in my stomach made the memory come roaring back, of my thighs sticky with cum and my skin plastered with sweat. The feel of her soft skin sliding under my hands felt like a distant dream, but I should have realized it as soon as I touched her. What kind of idiot was I?

"Kat, I'm sorry. I'm so sorry about all this." As soon as the words left my lips, something changed in the air between us. A tautness that seemed to stretch for miles, it echoed throughout the apartment and reflected back an unusual creak. My spine stiffened, drawing my shoulders back as every sense started screaming red alert danger signals. My gaze drifted over to Kat, the sound of her heartbeat kicking up a notch as she slipped towards the closet and grabbed an oversized hoodie. She pulled it over her head in a flash, and something else popped out of the pockets. Small and black, I could barely make out the outline of it against her hand, but the inner workings were snapping and popping like a live electric wire.

A stun gun, perfect.

Kat

"HERE, KITTY KITTY KITTY. I know you're here, or are you too busy fucking the mangy mutt to notice?" A voice straight out of my nightmares cooed. My hand tightened on my trusty little stun gun, squeezing the rubber grip until it squeaked between my fingers. Shit, he was here. In my own fucking apartment! I glanced toward Tyler, his body soundlessly easing towards the door without the help of his cane. I guess the overhead light was bright enough that he could decently see his way, but a small flash of fear still gnawed at my heart. "Where are you at, Kitty Kat? I just want to talk to you." Ronan called again, his whispers much louder this time.

"Keep quiet." Ronan's lips formed out the words without a sound, and he pressed his broad frame back against the wall like a curtain. Both sets of fingers spread wide like searching tentacles, and his bare feet planted firmly on the floor. He tilted his chin, aiming a quick bob of his chin towards the closet, and the subtle message clicked in my head. Hiding in the closet seemed like a shitty move right out of a bad horror movie, but it was the only thing I had that would work with me.

"Don't be stupid!" I hissed back in a whisper, hoping that Ronan wasn't close enough to hear me, and Tyler just flashed a reckless smile. Shit! He was going to fight him. The thud of footsteps deepened, the extra squeaky spot at the beginning of the hall shrieking out a warning, and I darted back into the closet as much as my belly would allow. The baby decided it must not have liked the imminent danger part, its tiny little feet aiming blow after blow to my lungs as the head punched down against my crotch. Bolts of bright white lightning flashed behind my eyes, the air completely rushing out of my chest, and my back bowed over to curl around my belly. "Stop it!" my teeth grated against one another, popping gunfire loud in my head as a few bitter tears stung my eyes.

The baby didn't stop, or rather, my muscles decided to turn into those iron bands again. My belly tensed under my hands, squeezing in on itself with the force of a contraction. Shit to fucking hell! My left eye winched up in pain, the floor rumbling beneath my feet as two large bodies repeatedly smacked into it. Curses that would have made a sailor proud filled the air, and punctuated with the wet smack of flesh and bone meeting flesh.

"Think you can win, little gimp mutt?" Ronan's voice was much higher than it was before, and thick too. Nasal, that's what the word was. Very nasal. Gritting my teeth, I leaned forward to peep through the crack of the door. Ronan's face matched his voice, a curtain of crimson blood had gushed over his lips, and still dripped from the broken slant of his nose that was tilted about 20 degrees off its normal angle. He flexed one meaty hand, the knuckles scrubbed raw, and aimed a punch for a blurred figure.

Tyler, moving at the limits of his wolf speed, blurred with a backflip onto the bed, landing easily in a fighter's crouch on the balls of his feet. A shimmer of golden eyes and half formed wolf muzzle accompanied the silky fur that raced down his shoulders, matted into thick clumps from fresh blood but I couldn't tell if it was his or Ronan's. The change partially underway, the nails on his hands had lengthened into talon like claws, turning each finger into a lethal weapon all its own. "There's no question about it. I'm going to win." His speech was much better than mine in wolf form, still able to sound like real words and everything. With Ronan between us like some kind of living wall, he leaned aside just enough that I could see his golden eyes and blinked slowly. His left hand twitched, briefly flaring flat out like he was pushing against an invisible wall.

My lips twitched up in a smile, the pain of the contraction momentarily forgotten as my wolf stirred up. The promise of winning the fight had her excited, a tingling surge of energy burning a familiar trail through my veins, and I steadied my grip on my stun gun. I had one shot, so I couldn't miss.

With a spine-chilling howl, Tyler charged forward. Driving Ronan back with a tackle worthy of a prizewinning linebacker, he looped both arms around Ronan's meaty waist and kept his head down. The budding growth of wolf pointed ears were slicked down to his skull, each long stride shoving him backwards and carrying Ronan completely off his feet.

They smacked against the wall just to my left, the closet shuddering against my back like it was about to crumple like old paper, and I sucked in a quick breath. Snaking out the door, I jammed the stun gun against his shoulder. "Have a nice nap, bozo!" I snarled in his ear, seeing Tyler leap back out of the corner of my eye, and I pushed the button.

I was told when I bought the stun gun for my personal protection that it could make for some pretty disturbing sights, but Ronan dropped without a sound. No twitches, groans, eyes bulging out of their sockets, or shaking limbs. Nothing at all like what they showed in the movies. Instead, his legs crumpled up like a doll's and he just tipped forward, falling flat onto his stomach with his arms starfished out to the sides. "Was that it?" Tyler growled low, his wolf ears twitching to catch any rousing sounds, but Ronan was quiet and perfectly still except for breathing. "Is he dead?"

"Nope, still breathing." I bent forward to check and almost toppled over on my head from the weight of my belly, but he was just fine. Knocked out, but fine. "Let's get Dom and throw this asshole back in jail where he belongs!"

"YOU DO KNOW THIS TUX was a rental, right?" Tyler's laugh rumbles through my palms as my fingers get to work shredding his buttons. I don't listen to him, my lips currently attached to his neck and worrying a collar of reddish blooms into his skin. He's mine now, and I intend to make sure that everyone knows it.

"So what? It's our honeymoon. They can go fuck themselves over a few missing buttons." Like the baby was answering me, a hearty kick to my belly had the white satin of my wedding gown rippling with the movement. Folded like a Grecian toga around one shoulder, the plunging neckline showed off the deep v of my cleavage but also draped nice and roomy around my belly. It wasn't easy to find a wedding dress for a 40 week + five days pregnant woman, and the challenge was doubled due to my height, but it actually turned out rather nice.

'You're so vicious while you're pregnant. It's hilarious." He laid a hand under my jaw, gently tilting my face back for a quick kiss. I smiled against his lips, dropping one hand between us to cup his throbbing cock that was pressing against the front of his well fitted black pants. Our whirlwind wedding had taken two weeks to prepare after Ronan was finally hauled away into jail, where he's securely awaiting trial with no permanent damage whatsoever from either his fight with Tyler or my stun gun. I was a little disappointed at that, but his brain was already fucked up enough so I suppose it doesn't matter. Then the wedding was delayed another two weeks because of both of us catching a cold, but now here we are. Me, overdue and huge, but now I have a little gold band on my finger and a hunky new hubby to go with it.

"Says the man who nearly shoved my ex through a wall, twice." A raspy chuckle buries itself in the skin of my breasts as he drops to his knees. One dark eye folds up in a playful wink, mimicking the red-hot tongue that laps slowly at my exposed cleavage. My hands latch onto his shoulders, the ebony painted tips curling deep into the fabric and firm muscle below. He doesn't flinch one bit, palming a hand over the curve of my belly on his way down lower.

"I had to protect what is mine." He said simply, nuzzling his cheek in the junction of my hip and my ribs. A surge of affection swelled in my chest, the kind of romantic rose petal throwing and butterfly causing sickness that could have made me barf any other time. But now... Now I just wanted to show him just how much he meant to me.

"Come here, Mr. Ferguson." I crooked a finger under his chin, hiking my skirt up with my other hand, and bopped him gently on the chin with my belly. Smiling so broadly that it stretched my lips from ear to ear, a small wriggle inside confirmed that all three of us were finally happy and together.

Don't miss out!

Visit the website below and you can sign up to receive emails whenever Talia Swarky publishes a new book. There's no charge and no obligation.

https://books2read.com/r/B-A-TGFK-TZTTB

BOOKS2READ

Connecting independent readers to independent writers.

Did you love *The Blind Alpha's Pregnant Mate*? Then you should read *Triple The Surprise*[1] by Talia Swarky!

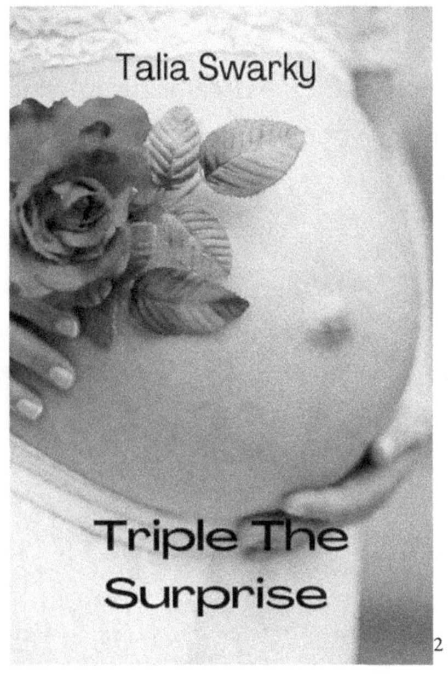

[2]

A collection of three rapid pregnancy inspired erotic tales. It all begins with the fan favorite of Brandi's unexpected surprise pregnancy via a pan of magical brownies, as witnessed by her fellow office workers in **Brandi's Brownie Baby Surprise.** Then, the entirely new story of **Tea for Two**, has Amanda eagerly awaiting the quickly arriving birth of her little one with her phone showing every moment to her fiancée. Finally, the tale of spunky Mandy planning an anniversary surprise for her hard working boyfriend Sebastian, but the pizza and lemonade she eats gives her a larger gift than what she had expected. Triplets to be precise in **Pepperoni Pizza And A Date Night Triplet Surprise.**

Read more at https://books2read.com/ap/nBkZpK/Talia-Swarky.

---

1. https://books2read.com/u/49Nrqw

2. https://books2read.com/u/49Nrqw

About the Author

A lover of the sensual side of things with a twist of fantasy, she is a writer of dreams and fantasies.

You can connect with her on Tumblr at https://midnightfantasiesanddaydreams.tumblr.com/

Read more at https://books2read.com/ap/nBkZpK/Talia-Swarky.